LEGENDS & FOLK TALES
OF
HOLLAND

Om aan je kinderen
mooie verhalen voor te lezen
uit ons Vaderland ....

Ome Philip

12 - 4 - 2003

LEGENDS & FOLK TALES

OF

HOLLAND

told by Adèle De Leeuw

ILLUSTRATED BY PAUL KENNEDY

HIPPOCRENE BOOKS, INC.
New York

Hippocrene Books, Inc. edition, 1999

Previously published in 1963 by Thomas Nelson & Sons.

ISBN 0-7818-0743-3

For information, address:
HIPPOCRENE BOOKS, INC.
171 Madison Avenue
New York, NY 10016

Printed in the United States of America

*In loving memory of
my father, A. Lodewyk De Leeuw,
friend, companion, and delightful
teller of tales*

The author wishes to express her gratitude for their generous help, given without stint, to Ruth P. Tubby, Director of the Montclair, New Jersey, Free Library; to Dorothy Jones, Reference Librarian, and O'Celia White, Children's Librarian, of the Plainfield, New Jersey, Public Library, and to Els van der Poort, Children's Librarian, Gemeente Bibliotheek, Rotterdam, The Netherlands.

Contents

THE DRAGON OF UTRECHT   11

THE EMPEROR'S QUESTIONS   15

THE SHOEMAKER'S DREAM   21

THE MERMAN'S REVENGE   28

DOUBLE AREND OF MEEDEN   33

THE ORDEAL OF LEYDEN   38

STORIES ABOUT KAMPEN   46

THE GOLDEN HELMET   52

THE KING'S RICE PUDDING   57

SUMMER SNOW   60

A LEGEND OF SAINT NICHOLAS   66

EMMA OF HAARLEM   71

THE CAT-CHALICE OF VLAARDINGEN   75

THE HAUNTED HOUSE   81

WHY PIGS ROOT   89

THE MISERLY MILLER   92

THE POFFERTJES PAN   97

JAN THE EIGHTH VAN ARKEL   101

THE KNIGHT OF STEENHUISHEERD   104

WHY BEARS EAT MEAT   109

THE MAN IN THE MOON   112

THE HOUSE WITH THE HEADS   114

THE PUNISHMENT   119

THE SIMPLE MAID OF HUNSINGOO   127

THE RICH WIDOW OF STAVOREN   133

THE SHELL GROTTO OF NIENOORT   139

THE CURSE   146

THE TWO WISHES   152

LEGENDS & FOLK TALES
OF
HOLLAND

❧ The Dragon of Utrecht ❧

MANY CENTURIES AGO there were dragons in Holland. No one knew just where a dragon might be found, but people did know that hens' eggs were sometimes laid without yolks, and such an egg might contain a young dragon, if it were hatched by a turtle on a dunghill. When the shell broke open a young dragon would come forth, such a frightful monster that everyone fled at its approach.

Now it was well known, too, that the eyes of dragons shot forth flames which could kill anyone who looked at them. In fact, the flames were so deadly that the dragons themselves were afraid of them. That was why they always tried to live in some dark place, like a pit or a deep, deep cellar.

There were endless tales of how men had been killed when

they came upon a dragon unexpectedly. Generally only one look was enough but if, by some odd chance, the man still lived after gazing at a dragon's eyes, the monster would poison him with the sharp spines that stood along its back.

In Dokkum alone eighteen people had been killed by dragons, and the body of a dragon had been found in a cave near Oldenoorde. How many people had perished there was not known, but when a dragon was discovered in Utrecht, everyone was up in arms. Something had to be done about it, and at once!

The dragon was found in this way: A brewer sent one of his servants to the deepest cellar to fetch some malt, and when the man didn't come back, he sent another servant to see what was the matter. This poor fellow found his companion dead, and he was going to call for help when, suddenly, he was face to face with a dragon. The flaming eyes seared him, and he clutched his heart with the pain. "Now, I, too, must die," he thought, and fell to the ground, lifeless.

When the second servant did not return, the brewer knew that both men must be dead, and the news spread that it could only have been a dragon that killed them. The people of Utrecht were terrified. "What are we going to do?" they cried. "Who will kill the dragon?"

A young man spoke up. "I will," he said firmly.

They laughed at him. "You! You're too young. You don't know what you're talking about."

"I will never dare go into my cellar again," the brewer said sadly. "And no one else will go, either. I shall be ruined."

"I will kill the dragon," the young man said again, still more firmly.

"How can you? What do you know about dragons?"

"I know how to kill them," he said. "At least, let me try."

"Do you realize that you may be killed, too?"

"Of course I do."

"And what will you kill him with? You have no sword, you have no bow and arrow. You don't even have a sling as David did when he killed Goliath."

"Just the same, I think I can kill him."

"With what?" the people insisted. "You are foolish and young—and stupid as well."

"I will go home and get my weapon," he said. And with that he departed. Everyone waited for him to come back. When he returned he had no weapon, no armor of any kind, only a board slung around his neck on a rope. It lay against his chest.

The people, in spite of their anxiety, hooted with laughter. "You're more stupid than we thought!" they jeered. "What makes you think a board—why, it isn't even a decent shield— will save you from the dragon?"

The young man took out a cloth and bound it over his eyes. "Now I will not be able to see him," he said calmly. "And if I do not see him, his eyes cannot frighten me, or kill me."

"But don't you realize he has huge spines along his back that can poison you?" they said. "And a dragon is so silent, even though he's huge, that he can move without your hearing him. How will you even know that he's near if you can't hear him and can't see him, with your blindfold on?"

The young man was tired of their talking and all their objections. "I said I would kill him. Wait and see," he said. And with that he went down the steps of the brewer's cellar and into the dark cave.

The dragon heard him coming and lifted his head. The young man moved forward cautiously. The dragon shot flames from his eyes and waited for him to fall dead. When he did not, the dragon shot still fiercer flames toward the oncoming figure. The young man heard the hissing of the flames and he laughed.

That infuriated the dragon. He crept forward in his noiseless fashion until he stood directly in front of the youth. No one had ever withstood him before. If this young man didn't die from the sight of the flames, then he must die from the poisonous spines along his back.

At that instant the young man grabbed the board that hung against his chest and turned it over.

It was a mirror! The dragon cried out with rage when he saw his own dreadful eyes in the glass.

The flames that shot forth from them were so fierce that he could not withstand them, and he fell, writhing in pain, and was burned to ashes.

And that is how Utrecht was freed from the terrible dragon. But what the name of the young hero was, the story doesn't tell.

≱ *The Emperor's Questions* ≰

ONE DAY when Charles V was walking in the Netherlands, which was part of his empire, he came upon an abbey. Over its gate he saw some words carved in stone. He stepped closer and read, "Here one lives without a care."

The emperor frowned. "How can that be? No one is free from care. I have the cares of half the world upon me. But even in a quiet place like this it seems impossible to live without any worry at all. I don't believe it. I must find out what the monks mean by that."

He sent for the abbot.

The abbot was a little man with a round face and merry eyes. When he got the message, he wasn't exactly *worried*— for his conscience was clear and he was a cheerful man—but he couldn't help wondering what the emperor wanted of him. After all, he was only a poor abbot, the head of a small abbey, and Charles V was ruler of the entire Holy Roman Empire!

He trotted down the road to the inn where the emperor was staying and bowed himself into the ruler's presence.

"Sire," he said, bending low, "you asked to see me?"

"So I did," said the emperor. "I wanted to see for myself a man who lives without a care."

"Not only I, sire, but all my monks," said the abbot with a smile.

"How can such a thing be?" The emperor was frowning.

"Why, it's a simple matter, sire. We eat and drink and sleep and pray, and we worry over nothing. There is nothing to worry about!"

"In a world full of care, it is wrong for even one person to live as you say you do. I cannot permit it. If you have nothing to worry about, I can give you something. You must learn what it is to fret and fume and turn problems inside out."

The abbot could not imagine what was coming.

"So I command you," the emperor said majestically, "to bring me the answers to these three questions by tomorrow morning, or suffer the consequences."

"Yes, sire?" the abbot asked.

"The first question is: What is the depth of the sea?"

The abbot repeated, "What is the depth of the sea?"

"The second question is: How many cows' tails would it take to reach from the earth to the sun?"

The abbot turned pale. This was getting worse and worse. But he repeated faithfully, "Yes, sire, how many cows' tails would it take to reach from the earth to the sun?"

"And the third question," said the emperor, with a smile that sent shivers down the abbot's back, "is what am I thinking about?"

"What are you thinking about?" the abbot repeated, despair filling his soul.

"And I want the answers by tomorrow morning, mind you, or it will go hard with you," the emporer reminded him. "Now go—and find out what it means to have trouble in this world."

The poor abbot plodded back to his abbey with slow steps and his head bent in thought. How would he ever find the answers to such impossible riddles? What had he done, or not done, on this earth, that he should be plagued by such dreadful questions? How could he even try to find the answers? He turned in at the gate over which the words were carved in stone, "Here one lives without a care."

"Alas," he thought sorrowfully, "that will never be true again."

The abbot paced up and down the halls. He walked back and forth in his little cell. He racked his brains, repeating the questions over and over again, praying heaven that he might know the answers before the morrow.

It was up to him to save his abbey and the monks who, until this day, had dwelt in it so happily. But what could he do, if he did not know the answers, or even how to go about finding them?

When he could stand it no longer, he went outside to walk in his garden. At any other time the beauty and quiet of the garden would have brought solace to him, but now the flowers and the birds and the whispering trees seemed to mock him. "How deep is the sea?" he kept hearing with every breeze. "How many cows' tails . . . what am I thinking?"

When the garden became unbearable to him, the abbot went across the fields, where he had always found peace in the past. But now the green grass, the grazing sheep, and the sunshine seemed to mock him, too.

He walked with his head bent so that he did not see the

shepherd until he was upon him. The shepherd was a small man, with a round face and merry eyes.

The shepherd said, "You look sad, Reverend Abbot. And I have never seen you look sad before."

"Misfortune has fallen upon me, and upon all of us," the abbot said dolefully. "Pity me."

"We have always been happy here," the shepherd said, puzzled. "What misfortune can have come to us since this morning?"

So the abbot told him of the emperor's impossible questions. "I must have the answers by tomorrow morning," the abbot said, "or evil will befall us. And how can I have all the answers by then? My brain has twisted and turned like a fox running before the hounds, but I can't think of an answer to a single question."

The shepherd did not seem to think the situation was too serious. "Why bother yourself about so small a thing as this?" he asked the abbot. "Leave it to me."

"How can I leave it to you?" the abbot said, a little crossly. "I must have the answers—and I can see no way of getting them."

"Well, that's why you must leave it to me," the shepherd replied. "Tomorrow I will dress myself in your robe and go to see the emperor. I have a feeling that all will come out well."

At first the abbot would not hear of it. "He asked *me*, and I am responsible," he said. "What's more, if *you* do not have the answers either, things will go even harder with us. No, I cannot allow it."

"But don't you see," the shepherd said, "if you don't know the answers, someone must go and give them to the emperor, and why not your humble shepherd? Now, Reverend Abbot, go in to your supper and do not give the matter another thought. Just let me wear your robe tomorrow."

"Well," the abbot said, after a long silence, "things could scarcely be worse. But I warn you, if the emperor is displeased, he will be mightily displeased. I tremble to think what will happen to us."

Since he could really do nothing else, the abbot had to let his shepherd dress in his clothes the next morning and go into the village where the emperor was staying. The shepherd was ushered into his presence and bowed low.

"My dear abbot," the emperor said with a smooth smile, "you have come to answer the questions I propounded to you?"

"So I have," the shepherd agreed.

"Let us start with the first one. How deep is the sea?"

"As deep as a stone's throw."

The emperor looked a little surprised. "That, of course, was a simple question. Now for the second one: How many cows' tails would it take to reach from the earth to the sun?"

"Sire, it would take only one, if it were long enough."

The emperor seemed quite startled. "True, true. Although I

had not thought of it quite that way. However, I wonder if you will be able to answer the third question. That is the most difficult of all." He leaned forward and looked piercingly at the shepherd. "Tell me, what am I thinking?"

The shepherd answered promptly. "O, sire, you are thinking at this moment that I am the abbot. But I am not. I am only his shepherd."

At that Charles V, Emperor of the Holy Roman Empire, burst into a fit of laughing. He laughed until his crown fell off. He laughed until he rocked in his chair. He laughed so hard and so long that all his courtiers came running, and when they saw him laughing they laughed, too, although they did not know why.

When he could finally speak, the emperor said, "The abbot is a fortunate man. Go back to the monastery, shepherd, and tell him that from now on he and his monks may well live without a care, because of you."

≫ The Shoemaker's Dream ≪

MEINDERT WAS A SHOEMAKER who lived across the street from the big church in the small village of Oosterlitten. He was a good man who worked hard from morning till night, but he never had very much money. He wished he could make enough to put some aside for the time when he and his wife Nelletje would be old. He wished he could buy an easy chair for himself and a handsome lace cap for Nelletje.

Once in a while he would lean back and close his eyes and dream of all the things he could do if only he had a little money.

"Dreams never get you anywhere," Nelletje said. "We're not badly off. Of course, it would be nice if I had new curtains, and I could do very well with a big brass pot like Mevrouw

21

Roelen's, but after all we have enough to eat, and the house is snug."

"Just the same, I can't help wishing—"

"You'd better stop wishing and get to work. The dominie's shoes will never be ready at this rate."

Meindert said nothing. But while he worked on the pastor's shoes, he went back to his wishing. And that night he had a strange dream.

"Do you know what I dreamed last night?" he said excitedly to Nelletje the next morning. "Someone said to me—"

"Who was it?"

"How do I know? I had never set eyes on him before. But he said to me, just as clearly as you're speaking to me now, 'Go to the Papenbrug in Amsterdam. You'll find a fortune there.' "

His wife held up her hands. "Now, that's nonsense! I'd never believe a stranger in the first place. And why the Papenbrug? Why would you find a fortune there—on a bridge?"

"I don't know," Meindert said stubbornly. "But that is what I dreamed and that's what I'm going to do."

"It costs money to go to Amsterdam. Besides, you've never been there. You'd get lost."

Meindert clamped his lips shut. That night he had the same dream again. He could talk of nothing else, and Nelletje grew cross with him.

"Only fools believe in dreams! Get on with your work or we'll go hungry this week."

There was something in what she said, and Meindert picked up his awl and set to work. But his thoughts were not on shoe-making.

When he had the same dream for the third time, his mind was made up. Nelletje cried, "You'll never get this out of your head until you *go* to Amsterdam, and find what a silly fool you've been! I'll pack you a lunch, but if you get lost, don't say I didn't warn you."

It was a long journey to Amsterdam. Meindert first had to take a boat across the Zuider Zee, and the water was very rough. He felt unhappy and seasick. Should he turn back? But how could he? He had already spent half of his money for the fare.

When he reached the bustling city of Amsterdam, he was bewildered, just as Nelletje had said he would be. There were so many streets, and so many canals, and so many, many bridges. How would he ever find the bridge called the Papen-brug? No one had time to answer his questions. He dodged the oncoming carriages and drays. People pushed him out of the way impatiently. He was shoved and jostled.

But at last he found one man who would listen to him. "The Papenbrug? You're standing on it!" The man gave Meindert a scornful look and hurried off.

Meindert thought, "Why, it looks like any other bridge! What's so different about it? How could I find a fortune here?"

He leaned over the coping and saw the reflection of his face in the water. Maybe Nelletje was right, and he was foolish to have come. A dog pulling a milk-cart bumped into him and nearly knocked him off his feet. The driver yelled at him, "Get out of the way, old man!"

Meindert left the bridge and wandered sadly through the streets nearby. He did not want to get too far from the bridge. There were still some hours to spend before his boat made the return trip. He would try once more before he went home.

Towards evening he went back to the bridge again. There seemed to be even more people on it than before. Why had he ever believed that he could find his fortune here? What sport Nelletje would make of him when he returned!

While he stood disconsolately fingering the few coins in his pocket, a ragged beggar came up to him. Meindert thought, "He's going to ask me for money, and I have only enough for my ticket home."

The beggar said, "Excuse me, mijnheer, but I've seen you near here all day. Maybe I can help you. Are you looking for something—or somebody?"

Meindert was so glad to hear a friendly voice that he said eagerly, "I had a dream that told me to come here."

The beggar laughed. "Who believes in dreams? *I* don't! Why, in the dream I had last night some silly fellow told me to go to Oosterlitten and find the big church. There would be a shoemaker living across the street, he said, and in his garden I would find a pot of coins. Now, who would be stupid enough to believe a thing like that?"

The shoemaker could barely wait to say a civil good-bye to the beggar. He hurried back to the boat, and paced up and down impatiently until it took off. The trip seemed even longer than it had in the morning, but he was so eager to be home now that he forgot to be seasick.

It was dark when he reached his house, but Nelletje was waiting up for him. "Well?" she greeted him, "did you bring home a fortune?"

"No, but I know where one is! Fetch a lantern, quickly, while I get the shovel."

"What are you going to do?"

"There's a pot of coins in the garden, and I'm going to dig it up."

"Have you taken leave of your senses? I knew that journey to Amsterdam would do you no good."

"Stop talking, woman, and fetch the lantern," Meindert ordered. In a fever of excitement, he went out into the cold garden. Nelletje, keeping up a running fire of derisive remarks,

held the lantern high. Meindert dug and dug. Perspiration streamed off his face, and his back felt broken.

"Come to bed, you silly man," Nelletje urged.

Just then his shovel struck something hard. He dug faster, and bit by bit uncovered a big iron pot. When he tried to lift it out, it was too heavy for him. Nelletje put down the lantern to help him. Now she was as excited as he was.

The pot was full of silver pieces. When they carried it into the house and counted the money, Meindert cried, "We have more than enough to buy an easy chair for me, and a lace cap for you, and new curtains, and a brass pot!"

Nelletje said, "But we'll not be rich! You'll still have to work!"

They stacked the coins in neat piles, and Nelletje scrubbed the dirt-encrusted pot until its black sides were spotless. "There's writing on it," she said. "But I can't make out what it says."

Meindert studied the strange characters. "I can't, either. Well, it doesn't matter."

"Then I'll hang it in the fireplace," Nelletje said. "I've always wanted a pot hanging in the fireplace."

When the dominie came for his shoes, Nelletje asked him to stay for a cup of tea. As he stretched his feet toward the peat fire, he said, "That's a fine pot you have hanging there. Where did you get it?"

Nelletje opened her mouth, but Meindert said quickly, "I bought it from a traveling tinker. There's writing on it. It's nothing we can read, though."

The dominie got up and peered at the pot. "I can read it," he said after a moment. "It's in a foreign tongue. But it makes no sense."

"What does it say?" Meindert and Nelletje asked with one voice.

"It says 'There is a bigger one beneath me.' Yes, I'm sure that's what it says." The dominie sounded puzzled.

"No matter," said Nelletje. She was anxious now for the dominie to leave. "Drink up your tea. It's getting dark."

As soon as he was gone, Nelletje lit the lantern and led her husband into the dark garden. "This is the very spot. I remember how we smoothed the earth over the hole. Dig deeper, Meindert."

The shoemaker bent willingly enough to his task. The mound of earth grew until it was over his head and he was standing in a deep hole. At last his shovel struck something hard. The strange words on the pot were true. It was another iron pot! And it *was* bigger than the first one!

Nelletje helped him lift the pot and drag it into the house. This time the coins were gold! When they had counted the money, they knew they were rich. There was so much money that Meindert could close his shop and live as well as a rich burgher. They could even move to Amsterdam.

"Who believes in dreams now?" he asked Nelletje in triumph.

"Well," she said, "in that *one* dream."

"Do you know what I'm going to do first?" he asked.

"Buy yourself a fine broadcloth suit," his wife suggested.

"Time enough for that," said Meindert. "First, I will go to Amsterdam and hunt the city over until I find that poor beggar who didn't believe in *his* dream, for he made mine come true. I will give him enough money to keep him in comfort the rest of his life."

≽ *The Merman's Revenge* ≼

Long, long ago there was a fishing port on the lovely island of Walcheren. Proud ships sailed out of the harbor of Westerschouwen, traveling far and wide on the North Sea and bringing home rich cargoes. The people of the town grew prosperous and haughty. There was no port to equal theirs, no ships better than theirs. They felt that they were the rulers of the sea, and they bragged loudly, to anyone who would listen, that their fishermen were the finest in the world.

One day some fishermen of Westerschouwen let down their net and when they pulled it up they drew back in astonishment.

"A mermaid!" they cried. "We've caught a mermaid!"

In the net cowered a lovely creature. Her golden hair fell

over her face, and her slim, fishlike body was covered with green scales.

She begged them, with tears in her eyes, "Let me go! Please, please let me go!"

"Let you go!" one of the men jeered. "What do you think we are? A prize like this will make us the best-known fishermen in the land. Shall we take her back to Westerschouwen, eh, mates, and show her to the people? No one would believe us otherwise."

"Aye, aye, we'll take her back and show her!" the others cried.

The poor mermaid was in despair. "Let me go! I will die on land. If you let me go back to my home, you will be blessed a thousand times!"

"What blessing do we need?" they shouted. "We don't need rewards. A catch like this is reward enough for anyone!" And they crowded around and laughed and poked at her while she trembled in the strong net.

Suddenly another voice came from the sea beside the boat. It was deep, and filled with sorrow.

"Let my wife go!" the voice begged.

"A merman!" the fishermen cried in excitement. "Let's catch him, too! What a prize!"

But they could not catch the merman. He always swam just out of their reach. When he rose from the waves they saw that he carried a child, a tiny mermaid, in his arms. The merman's hair was as green as the sea and flowed over his foam-covered shoulders. His face was the color of a piece of driftwood.

The mermaid heard her husband and struggled in the net, holding out her white hands to the firshermen. "Let me go, let me go!"

The merman's deep voice called, "Give her back to me. We

were so happy in our little home made of shells and seaweed. Together we gathered the shells for our house. She cannot live on land—she will die. And her baby needs her!"

But the fishermen laughed. "Swim away, merman, or you will be in our net, too!"

When they reached port, they made their ship fast and hurried ashore with their treasure. The townsfolk came running to see the strange, beautiful creature they had caught in their net. The mermaid wept and hid her face behind her golden hair, and she trembled with fear as they peered at her.

"Let's take her to the tower and tie her there!" the people said. "Then she can't get away and we can come and look at her any time we want to."

The poor mermaid was imprisoned in the tower. The merman swam as close to it as he could. "Give her back to me, give her back to me!" he entreated. "Or you will rue this day!"

But the fisherfolk laughed all the harder. "We're not afraid of you! What could you do to us? You have no fire, you have no sword, you have nothing to hurt us with. Begone!"

At last, the mermaid died, and the merman swam away with his child in his arms. His heart was filled with sorrow, and with rage. "I have a weapon," he thought. "I have a weapon mightier than fire or sword."

After he had taken his child under the water to the pretty house made of shells, he returned to the harbor of Westerschouwen. He dived deep and brought up seaweed and sand. He filled up the channels where the ships were wont to go. In a few hours the waterways were choked with sand and weeds. The fisherfolk heard his voice, like a wailing wind far away, singing:

> Oh, fishermen of Westerschouwen,
> You will rue the day
> When you took my lovely

Mermaid-wife away.
Now all the town of Westerschouwen
Shall drownéd be in sand,
And only the tall tower
Where she died shall stand.

No one believed the words of the strange song. But they were true. Like a tide that cannot be stopped, the sand and the weeds came closer and closer. Winds and storms came and drove the sand inward. The fishing boats could not get out to sea; their hulls were tangled in the seaweed. With every wind sand blew over the town of Westerschouwen. It piled up on the streets; it surrounded the buildings. The sand was everywhere. It swept through the doors and along the walls. It filled the rooms of all the houses. It fell on the roofs until they collapsed. The frantic people fled the town, but the wind still blew the sand. It covered the ships and the trees and the houses—until no one could know that a ship or a house had ever been there.

The merman had sung true. The tower where his wife had died was spared. Lonely and tall, it stood against the blue sky, with the green water of the sea lapping at its feet—all that remained of the proud port where the cruel people of Westerschouwen had lived.

❧ Double Arend of Meeden ❧

WHEN HE WAS STILL A CHILD, Double Arend was as strong as a bull and as quick as a flea. All the boys of the village went out of their way to avoid him, and no one had to ask who was the strongest lad in Meeden. His muscles were twice as thick, his hands and neck twice as large and his shoulders twice as broad as those of boys of his own age, and he had a voice twice as loud.

At sixteen, he could fight men of twenty, *two at a time,* and lay them on the ground with one blow. By his nineteenth birthday, he could fight four at once—and win. Men from Muntendam, and Zuidbroek, and Scheemda heard about him and couldn't believe Double Arend was as strong as people said he was. But it turned out that he wasn't afraid of fighting three from Scheemda, or four from Mutendam, or five from Zuidbroek, at one time.

When it was time for Double Arend to take a wife, he went to Winschoten, a nearby town. A young woman named Elsa who lived there pleased him very much. She ate clabbered cream and bacon for early breakfast, pea soup with ham and thick pancakes for her midday meal, and brown beans and barley pudding for supper. Double Arend married her, and she became the mistress of his cottage.

As soon as Elsa was settled in her new home, she began to plague her husband by nagging him. She would even wake him up in the night to listen to her complaints. If he answered her, it made her angry, and if he didn't answer, it made her still angrier.

"It's easy enough to bring a wife into your house," Double Arend thought, "but it's another thing to keep her from talking."

One morning Elsa went to Winschoten, without telling her husband, and returned with her mother and father.

"My parents are going to live with us," she told Double Arend.

"I can't afford it," he replied.

"Then you'll just have to work harder," his wife said.

And so he did. Double Arend had to work from sunup till late at night. He did the work of ten men, and he didn't have enough to eat. Instead of a good thick sandwich of ham and cheese for his supper, his wife gave him only bits and pieces of leftovers, and he was so hungry he could barely sleep at night.

One day some time later, Elsa said to him, "Now that my father and mother are here, I think my two brothers and seven sisters should come to live with us."

"I can't afford it!" Double Arend cried.

"Then you'll just have to work harder."

Who knows how long this miserable existence would have gone on for poor Double Arend if his wife had not died suddenly?

After she was buried, he said to himself, "I wonder if her family will stay here, eating their heads off."

Sure enough, they stayed. Around his table sat her mother and father, her two brothers and seven sisters—all eating his food.

"Get out here, all of you!" Double Arend shouted. His voice shook the walls, and he lifted the table and all the chairs, with the people sitting on them, and set them down outside the house.

"There's no use crying over spilt milk," he said, "or over what has happened. That's past. I wish you a good journey back to Winschoten."

At last, Double Arend was master of his own house.

"No woman will ever cross my doorsill again," he said. And no woman ever did.

But that's not all they tell of Double Arend.

The farmers of Meeden had to pay taxes to the king. Everyone paid them except Double Arend. "I don't know the king," he said.

He refused to pay a penny, and the king wrote a letter to the judge in Winschoten, and he in turn gave it to the bailiff and told him to bring Double Arend to court. But as soon as the bailiff heard he had to arrest Double Arend, he got such a pain in his stomach that he had to stay in bed. Now the judge of Winschoten had no liking for the job, either, so he wrote a letter to the king, suggesting that His Majesty go to Meeden to tend to the matter himself.

The king got the letter early one morning, and at once gave the order to bring out his golden coach. He would show that farmer who was king!

The coachman forced the horses to make the trip from The Hague to Meeden without stopping, and when they reached the village the king asked all the people, even the children, to tell him where Double Arend lived. The villagers would not tell him; the truth was that they were more afraid of Double Arend's fists than they were of the king.

The king drove on and, at last, saw a lone man in a field, following his plow. Alighting from his coach, he walked up to him.

"My friend," said the king, "can you tell me where Double Arend lives?"

"What do you want with him?"

"I am the king, and I want to talk to him."

"What for?"

The king said sternly, "He owes me money, and I've come to collect it."

The man pointed to a little house across the field. "That's where Double Arend lives," he said. Then he put one hand under his horse's belly and lifted the horse *and* the plow high in the air. "And here stands Double Arend himself," he bellowed.

The king said, "So?"

And that was all he said. Now he knew why the bailiff of Winschoten had such a pain in his stomach. He ran to his golden coach, the coachman laid the whip on the horses, and the king rode back to The Hague as fast as he had come.

❧ The Ordeal of Leyden ❧

IT WAS IN THE MONTH OF MAY in the year 1574 that Valdez, the Spanish general, besieged the city of Leyden, for the second time. And because the burghers had not listened to the advice of Prince William of Orange to stock the city with supplies, they now saw the shadow of famine everywhere.

"Hold out three more months," the prince wrote, "and I will be able to help you."

In the city there was a tall tower. For weeks on end there was a constant stream of burghers going up the steps of the tower, to stare out over the surrounding meadows. They could see the ring of forts occupied by the Spaniards, and the spires of neighboring towns and villages. They could see the series of land-dikes which protected the countryside inside the great sea-dike. But they could see no ships coming from the prince. William of Orange was lying on a sickbed in Rotterdam, and his fever was made worse by his anxiety over the fate of Leyden. But he sent no word of his illness, either by messenger or by carrier pigeon, to the defenders of the fortified city. He was afraid that the people would lose heart if they knew how sick he was.

For two long months the people of Leyden had lived on brackish water and hard bread. And now, in the third month, they were wandering through the streets, hunting for anything that could be eaten.

"How can we believe the prince will free us?" the burghers asked each other. "For two months we at least had bread. Now we have nothing!"

"When you look from the tower you see the glitter of the sun on the Spaniards' weapons everywhere about us."

"The prince *can't* help us. He hasn't the army to win against Valdez's legions," said one burgher.

"Ours will probably be the fate of Naarden and Haarlem," replied another. Both of these cities had been pillaged, and the people had been herded into the churches and burned alive.

"But don't you remember what Valdez said in his letters to us? That he would promise us—"

"You can't trust a Spaniard's promises."

"We're hungry! We're hungry and our children are hungry!"

Finally someone said, "Let's go to the burgomeester and ask him to kill all the cows and horses, so that we will have something to eat."

"But who will be willing to give up his cow? Or his horse, either?"

The burgomeester and the town council decided that the

animals must be killed, but they would be drawn by lot. No one objected to this. First, the cows were killed, one by one. The meat was divided equally among the rich and poor, and for a short time the people's hunger was stilled.

Then, after all the cows had been killed, it was time to slaughter the horses. This was a real hardship, for the horses pulled the wagons, and carried folk around the city, and transported the vital supplies to the fortified walls. How could they be spared, even in this time of siege?

Barend, one of the burghers of Leyden, owned a horse that was as dear to him as a friend. Day and night he worried about the chance of his beloved Flink's being chosen by lot. Yet he knew he could not expect his horse to be spared. Every morning he dragged himself to the square where the lots were drawn, and morning after morning went by without his name being called. Later he would climb the worn steps of the tower to look out over the countryside.

On the west, toward the sea, the water was slowly beginning to rise, for the Prince of Orange had ordered the dikes to be pierced in a desperate attempt to save the city of Leyden. If the sea water flooded the low-lying fields, Admiral Boisot's fleet, the "Beggars of the Sea," might sail over them to meet and conquer the Spaniards. The "Beggars" were men who had sworn to defend Holland to the death. Now the land lay under a foot and a half of water, and the fleet was drawing near.

"But," Barend said to himself, "Valdez's troops are over there, and our men will never be able to break through. I am afraid Flink will be killed."

The next morning, however, when he came to the market square another man's name was read out. Overjoyed, Barend rushed back to the tower. Had the water come nearer? Yes, it had. Now Boisot's fleet perhaps could sail across it and reach the city.

But the wind blew the waters of the sea back, and where they had been deep, the ground began to rise above the tiny waves. A man standing beside Barend said, "The 'Beggars' will have to go through the canal to reach the lake!"

Barend saw that the canal was guarded by thousands of Spaniards. The Dutch fleet lay motionless in the low water, and when the ships tried to get through the canal, they ran aground. The wind still blew from the east, and the waters continued to recede. Soon the ships would be stranded on dry land.

The faces of the people of Leyden became thinner with worry and hunger. Seven days and seven nights this went on. And every morning Barend went to the market place. He would clench his fists until the knuckles showed white each time a name was called.

When he went home, he would throw his arms about Flink's neck. "They want to kill you," he would cry, "to save Leyden for the prince! But sometimes I ask myself if it wouldn't be better if Leyden were lost, and you were spared."

Then, on the eighteenth of September, the wind changed to the northwest. The waters rushed inland again. They rose and rose, and lifted up the ships. It was heartening to see how high the vessels rode.

The Spaniards at Zoetermeer and Benthuizen heard the waves washing against the dike between the two towns day and night, and they realized that their enemy's fleet would soon be upon them. They fled in panic. The Dutch fighters put both villages to the torch, and the fires that lit up the skies were a sign to their countrymen that victory might be near.

But they were jubliant too soon. When the fleet came to Noordaa, the waters receded again, and the ships were stranded once more. Despair filled their hearts.

Despair was in Barend's heart, too. "If the fleet has to stay long in Noordaa, it can only mean that my name will be drawn, for there aren't many horses left in Leyden," he thought sadly. "On the day that happens, I will not eat a bite, no matter how hungry I am. For I'd be afraid that even one drop of Flink's blood might be mixed in the food I ate."

The Prince of Orange knew how discouraged his people were. He rose from his sickbed to speak to the Beggars of the Sea aboard their ships. When they saw him, fierce fighters though they were, they rejoiced like children.

The prince had given his word that he would save the city, but it was hard for the people of Leyden to wait. Six thousand had died of the plague. Hunger stalked the streets and the people grew angry and restive. A great mob streamed toward the church of Saint Pancras where the burgomeester stood, and surrounded him, crying, "When is this going to end?" "Why must this happen to us?" "Is there nothing you can do?"

The burgomeester, Van der Werf, stepped forward. His face was drawn, his eyes fiery. He cried out in a strong voice, "What will it get you, my friends, if we break our word and let the city be taken by the Spaniards? If we do that, our fate will be worse than the one we are facing now."

Barend thought to himself, "Perhaps, if we surrendered, Flink would be spared."

Van der Werf's voice rose above the mutters of the crowd. "I have sworn to hold the city. I can die only once, whether it be by your hand, or by the hand of our enemies, or by the hand of God. It does not matter what happens to me. It does matter what happens to the city. I know that we shall die of hunger if Leyden is not soon relieved. But that is preferable to a dishonorable death. Your threats do not move me. Take my life! Here is my sword. Thrust it into my heart, and divide my flesh among you to satisfy your hunger. But do not expect me to surrender this city so long as it is in my hands."

His words lifted the people's spirits, and they resolved to hold out a little longer. But children died in the streets. Women tore the leaves off the trees and ate them. The pain of hunger gnawed at everyone's vitals.

On the twenty-eighth of September a carrier pigeon flew into the city, with a letter tied to its leg. "Be of good courage, burghers of Leyden," Admiral Boisot had written. "Only a few more days, and you will be rescued."

Barend said, "Boisot wrote 'only a few more days.' Perhaps my name won't be drawn, after all."

But the wind blew from the east, always from the east, on the twenty-eighth, the twenty-ninth, and the thirtieth of September. Would help never come?

"This endless east wind!" Barend muttered. "Only a couple

of horses are left in Leyden, and Flink will surely be put to death. I can't offer anybody money. What good is money in times like these? And yet I would give all I have if another could take his place."

Even on the first of October his name was spared. That night a storm swept out of the northwest, and a few hours later, from the southwest. All the waters of the sea seemed to gather together and race through the breached dikes and across the meadows, rising higher and higher, inch by inch. Boisot and his ships sailed across the land between the roofs and chimney pots of the submerged farmhouses.

That morning Barend rose early and struggled toward the tower through the storm. Rain poured over him but he scarcely noticed it. As he came to the market place, he heard a name being called. It was his!

He went back to his house and took Flink's reins in his hand. Slowly, they walked toward the slaughtering place. At the last moment, he held the horse's head close and cried, "It's not my fault, Flink! It's not my fault! But can you forgive me?"

The storm rose, and with it the water. Night came, and in the darkness there was a sudden terrific crash. People leaped from their beds in fright. Was it the Spanish army in a surprise attack?

They found that a whole section of the city wall had fallen, but there were no Spaniards to be seen. There were strange glimmering lights, like will-o-the-wisps, dotting the landscape. The people of Leyden did not know what the lights meant, nor what caused the clanking noises in the distance. But when day broke, a messenger came running from the forest at Lammen which the enemy had occupied. He called to the burghers. "The Spaniards are gone! The Spaniards are gone!"

No one would believe him, but when the burghers rushed

through the gates, they found that the encampment of the enemy had been deserted in the night. Not a Spaniard remained. The army had fled so hastily that the fires still burned under the iron pots filled with stew.

Leyden was saved! The people ran through the streets, embracing each other, and shouting. The church bells rang. The children danced on their thin little legs. The Beggars of the Sea, sailing across the meadows and up into the city, tossed bread and precious foodstuffs to the waiting throngs.

Only one man wept, and could not be comforted. Tears ran down Barend's cheeks. The city was saved, but his dear friend Flink was gone.

❧ Stories About Kampen ❧

I

ON A COLD WINTER'S DAY the councilmen of Kampen were
sitting around the hearth in a big room in the city hall. Their
heads nodded as they debated on this and that. They were in
no hurry to leave, for an east wind was blowing, and the wind
had no more mercy on members of the council than it had
on other people.

"What a storm!" one of the men said, shivering. "Last night
it froze harder than it has ever done before, and my wife's
aunt said this is the worst winter she has ever lived through.
That really means something, because next spring she'll be
seventy-eight years old!"

46

"Harrumph!" said the burgomeester, clearing his throat. "Let us call the servant and tell him to lay some more wood on the fire."

So the servant was called. He bowed low with a respectful air, but no one noticed it. "What may your lordships want?" he asked.

"We're cold," the mayor said, rubbing his hands together. "Put some more wood on the fire."

When the servant had built up the fire and the flames were dancing high up the chimney, the councilmen all moved closer to the hearth. The warmth was welcome to their cold bodies and brought a rosy glow to their hands which had turned white with the cold.

"It's better here than outside," the burgomeester said, and pulled his chair still closer to the hearth.

"Those are true words," the oldest member said importantly.

"I think so, too," the youngest member piped up.

"The next thing on the agenda," the burgomeester said, banging his gavel on the oak table nearby, "is the matter of the bridge."

"What bridge?" one of them asked.

"We must have a bridge here in Kampen." The mayor reproved him with a look. "Without a bridge we can't *cross* the bridge."

"And if there is no bridge here, the ships can't go *under* the bridge," one man said solemnly.

"And if it rains, the rain will fall in the water and not *on* the bridge," one councilman said.

"Sometimes you have to wait for a bridge to be let down, if it's open," another said gravely.

"And shipping always increases if there is a bridge," his neighbor added.

"And you can't walk over the water."

"And you can always fish from a bridge."

"And if you don't have a bridge, then you don't have a bridge."

"And it is useful for the future if there is a bridge," the burgomeester stated.

The oldest council member looked at him suspiciously and rubbed his nose. "What future?" he demanded.

Then the youngest council member spoke up in a voice loud and clear, and said everything in one question. "*What has the future ever done for us?*"

Everyone agreed that he had said something very profound. It was decided that until the future proved it was prepared to do something for the citizens of Kampen, they would not build a bridge that might be useful for the future.

Suddenly they all sniffed, and turned to one another in alarm. Smoke! They called loudly for the servant, and the burgomeester asked anxiously, "Is there a fire in the neighborhood?"

"No, your honor," the servant said. "But, if I may say so, the burgomeester's trousers are beginning to scorch."

"Aha! We shall have to do something about that!"

For a long time they all thought about it. The fire was not to be permitted to singe the burgomeester's trousers. But how could one prevent it? No one dared utter a word until the burgomeester had said his say.

"Honored members of the council of this city," he said at last, "the situation is one of peril. I, your burgomeester, can think of only one means of overcoming it."

Everyone waited breathlessly for his solution.

"Honored members of the council of this city," he repeated impressively, "the chimney must be built in the *rear* of the room instead of the *front* where it now is. If that is done, we shall have no more difficulty with the fire."

And that's what they did, at great expense and trouble.

But whether it helped, the story does not say. And neither does the story say whether the future ever showed what it would do for the citizens of Kampen so that they could decide about building a bridge.

II

ONCE A MAN who live in Kampen went to visit a friend in Amsterdam. They took a little walk while they talked of this and that.

The Amsterdammer said proudly, "My friend, I want you to note the spirit and intelligence—I might almost say the genius—of the Amsterdammers. Notice our sense of order and how well regulated everything is here. We have logic and insight, qualities shared by all our good burghers. Now, over there is the Bourse, where we Amsterdammers pump the gold out of the stupid provinces, so that we can ride in carriages. Work hard, my poor Kampenaar. You work for us! Catch fish in your River Ysel, sturgeon and pike—we like to eat both! Did you ever know that the hay you grow is for *our* horses? The butter and cheese you make is for *our* tables? As a matter of fact, the more I think of it, the more I realize that you Kampenaars are really a stupid lot. You might as well recognize it. What you do is stupid, and what we do is intelligent."

The Kampenaar frowned.

"Everything?"

"Everything," said the Amsterdammer firmly.

"Without exception?" the Kampenaar persisted.

"Without any exception."

The Kampenaar looked crestfallen. He sat down to think this over, but he sat down on a bench that had just been

painted. His friend pulled him up and wiped off his trousers, like a parent handling a helpless child. They walked on together.

The Kampenaar was still trying to think of something to say when they came to a small side street. There he saw a sight that made his mouth fall open in astonishment. He tapped his friend on the shoulder.

"Amsterdammer, Amsterdammer! Not all Amsterdammers are intelligent."

"Absolutely—without exception."

"Men and women?"

"Men and women. An Amsterdam sow has more intelligence than a Kampen alderman."

"Now wait a minute!" the man from Kampen shouted gleefully. "Just look at that maidservant over there. She's mopping down the steps. See—instead of beginning at the top she's working from the bottom up! Then she'll have to climb the steps with her dirty shoes and soil the steps she has just cleaned.

So her work goes for nothing. Does that show intelligence? Don't tell *me* that all Amsterdammers are bright!"

His friend waved his hands as if dismissing the subject. "Ask her where she was born," he said.

The Kampenaar went over to the maidservant and said, "I beg your pardon, miss, where do you come from?"

She turned around and looked at him in surprise. "Why, from Kampen, naturally," she answered, and went back to her work.

⚹ *The Golden Helmet* ⚹

LONG, LONG AGO there were no churches in Friesland. But in the woods were the sacred trees of the god whom the people worshipped most—Fosite, the God of Justice. The people thought the leaves of his tree were magical, and they brought their sick and wounded to lie under its branches to be healed.

The king of this country had a daughter whom he adored. He had named her for the god—Fostedina, or Lady of Justice. Her fair skin and long golden hair made her beautiful, and she was as kind and just as her name.

One day there came to the court a harper from the south. The courtiers listened to his songs and grew mightily angry. For he sang no stirring accounts of battles or of the killing of wild bears, or tales of vengeance and strife, but gentle songs of love and pity and understanding. He sang of a strange man called Jesus, who was the Son of God. He told His story and how, even on the cross where He had been hung wearing a crown of thorns, He had forgiven his enemies.

"Kill him!" the pagan priests shouted. "Who is this singer to tell us to forgive our enemies? Our enemies are the Danes! We will never forgive them! We will have vengeance on them!"

They rushed forward, and Fostedina, with tears in her eyes, flung herself in front of the harper and covered him with her golden hair.

The king stood up. "Stay your swords! This man is our guest. You must not harm him, or you yourselves will know death!"

The priests muttered among themselves. "The king must be under this man's spell!" they said. "How can he talk of forgiving the Danes?"

"What have the Danes done?" Fostedina asked her maidservant.

The maidservant said fearfully, "Did you not know? Some Danes came yesterday to our country. They had no arms. They came to tell of a man called Christ. It was cold in the woods where they camped and they cut branches from—from the tree to make a fire! The sacred tree of our god Fosite!"

"They did not understand," Fostedina murmured.

"It may be so. . . . But they have desecrated the sacred tree. They must die. They were captured and are in the dungeon now. Tomorrow they will be thrown into the wolf-pit."

Fostedina grew pale, but she said nothing—not even to her faithful maidservant. When it was night, she put a dark robe about her, and bound up her hair, and went stealthily to the dungeon. The men crowded in the low, cold, bare room could hardly believe their eyes. She took a key from under her robe and opened the great door.

"Go! Go in the name of the One the harper sang of. Return to your own country. I will show you how to get through the woods in the dark. Do not fear the bears and the wolves. You will be safe if you follow the path."

Fostedina led the Danes through the dark forest and set them on their way. She waited, shivering, while the wolves howled in the distance, but she knew the men would escape. Then she went back to the castle. And there the guards met her and led her to the king.

"Oh, my poor daughter!" he cried when he had heard her story. "How can I save you now?"

He knew that, in the morning, when the people learned that she had freed the prisoners, they would be furious. They had looked forward to the sport of baiting the wolves with the Danes. They would demand Fostedina's life.

In the morning she was brought before the priests. The chief priest called upon the gods to avenge them; he called down the curse of Wotan upon the princess. But she held her head high.

Her voice rang out clear and true. "Our dear Lord forgave His enemies. I will suffer as He did. I will not deny Him, no matter what you do to me!"

"You have sentenced yourself by your own words!" the chief priest said angrily. "You shall wear a crown of thorns, as they say that man did. You shall stand in the market place from morn to night, with the crown on your brow, and you will learn what it is to suffer!"

He thought that when Fostedina heard this she would beg for mercy; but she said not a word. Her father begged for mercy for her, but the priests said she must ask for it herself. And she would not.

The next morning she went to the market place. Her step

was firm and her head high. She was dressed in white furs and her golden hair fell over her shoulders.

The priest called for the crown of thorns. "This is for the one who has insulted our god Fosite! Kneel!" he ordered Fostedina.

She knelt before him, and the priest pressed the crown of thorns so hard upon her brow that the blood trickled over her forehead and down her cheeks.

He expected her to cry out, but she was silent. She rose and went to the center of the market place and stood there. The people milled around her, yelling and jeering at her. She did not move. They watched her quiet face, her half-closed eyes. She was praying to the God whom she had learned to know. "Forgive them," she prayed. "Teach me to forgive them, too."

All day she stood there, until darkness fell. The people got tired of their sport and went away. They were a little ashamed, too, of the way they had acted. They had always loved their king's daughter. If she believed so strongly in this new god, perhaps she knew something that they did not know.

Her maidservants washed the blood from Fostedina's face, but it took a long time for the wounds made by the thorns to heal. And forever after she bore the scars.

In the years that followed, the old king died, and Fostedina became Queen of Frisia. The people turned to her and she did not fail them. She told them of her God, and how kind and just he was. She built churches, and men came from the south to sing, as the harper had done, of the life of Christ. The people cut down the trees of their pagan gods, and turned the forests into meadows where flowers bloomed and cattle grazed. Churches dotted the landscape and their steeples, bright with crosses of gold, shone against the sky.

One fine day a prince rode into Frisia. He saw Fostedina and fell in love with her, and she with him. They were to be married and together reign over Frisia. On her wedding day a procession of maidens made their way to the castle. They carried a crown of gold, made in the form of a helmet, and they bowed low as they presented it to her.

"It is for you to wear," they said. "So that the scars of the dreadful thorns will not show."

Fostedina was touched; she let them put it gently on her head. And so she was married, wearing the golden helmet. And to this day the women of Frisia wear a helmet of gold, with a rosette of gold over each ear, the whole covered with a fine lace cap. They wear it proudly, for it is a memento of the days when the Frisians turned from their pagan gods to become Christians.

And when the Queen of the Netherlands visits her subjects in Friesland she, too, wears, for that day, a helmet of gold.

❧ The King's Rice Pudding ❧

IN THE LITTLE TOWN OF ONSTWEDDE there was great excitement. The king was coming to pay a visit!

The farmers gathered together to decide what they could do to honor him. Of course, they must give the king a gift. But what could they give him? He was very rich, and surely had everything he wanted, and they were only poor farmers.

At last the burgomeester cried, "I have it! Everyone says our wives make the best rice pudding in the world. Why don't we all give him a bowl of rice pudding?"

They thought this was a good idea, and every man went home to tell his wife to make the finest rice pudding she had ever made in her whole life.

When the great day came each farmer appeared at the town

hall, carrying his wife's most treasured bowl filled to the brim with rice pudding, rich with cream and sugar and sprinkled with nutmeg.

"Now," said one of the farmers, "we have the puddings. But how shall we present them? I, for one, have never had an audience with the king, and I'll wager none of you has, either."

The burgomeester said, "Don't let that bother you. I'll go first, and you follow me, and do just as I do."

When the doors of the town hall were thrown open the burgomeester, holding his bowl high, entered the audience chamber with stately steps. His robe of office swung from side to side. Just as he reached the foot of the dais where the king was sitting on a thronelike chair, he tripped on the hem of his robe and fell on his face. The bowl of pudding flew from his hands and broke into a hundred pieces on the highly waxed floor.

The king was startled, and he frowned at the rice pudding spattered on his royal garments. The farmer following the burgomeester thought this was a very strange way of greeting royalty. But the burgomeester had said to do whatever he did, so the farmer entered the room with solemn steps, advanced to the dais, and fell flat on his face, dropping his bowl of rice pudding at the king's feet.

The burgomeester was furious. "Oxhead!" he shrieked. "Lout! Oaf!"

The farmer got to his feet and turned to the king. "Oxhead!" he bellowed. "Lout! Oaf!"

The burgomeester was nearly out of his mind. He grabbed the farmer by the shoulder and boxed his ears. Whereupon the farmer turned to the next man and boxed *his* ears. This man boxed the next man's ears, and so it went, while the bowls

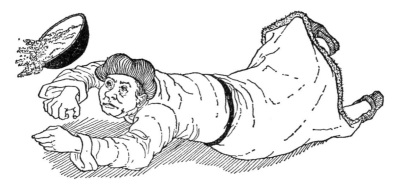

fell and broke spattering pudding all around the room, and men piled on top of each other in a free-for-all fight.

At first the king was astounded at this reception. Then, looking at the tumbling men with their clothes and hair covered with "the best rice pudding in the world", he burst out laughing. He laughed until his sides ached.

The burgomeester was so upset at the way his plans had gone awry that he caught the man nearest him, and dragged him from the room. The others picked themselves up and followed.

The burgomeester cried, "I'll never be able to hold up my head again."

But the king had never enjoyed himself so much. After he left the town he sent one of his couriers back with a purse filled with gold and a note. In the note the king said, "I have never been more amusingly entertained than in Onstwedde. Someday I must come back and *taste* 'the best rice pudding in the world.' "

⤳ Summer Snow ⤶

IN THE VILLAGE OF CANNE, a tall and beautiful linden tree stood near a hill, close to a tiny chapel. The seven aldermen of Canne always met under its spreading branches, and it was as if they were closed in a room. Neither sunlight nor rain could penetrate the tree's close-woven leaves. Whenever a person who had committed a crime was brought before the aldermen, he stood under the linden, and the onlookers ranged themselves in a circle around it.

A young widow named Josina lived in Canne. She was alone in the world except for her little son, and she had to work hard to support them both.

Unfortunately, there was someone in the village who wished

her ill. A man she had once refused to marry was forever spying on her, though Josina did not know this. Whenever she found work, she lost it almost at once because the man spread some malicious tale about her. At last she was obliged to seek work in the city.

Each morning when Josina left for Maastricht, she would kiss her son and tell him to be good while she was gone. "Be careful, dear," she would say, "and don't play near the Jeker. It is such a deep river." And the little boy would promise, and wave good-bye to her.

One afternoon when she came back from the city to the village of Canne, Josina saw people milling about her house. Her heart beat hard with sudden fear and she hurried toward them. They fell back silently and let her pass.

Josina saw with horror that her son lay on the cobblestones. His face was blue and his hair matted. Water still trickled from the corners of his mouth. He was dead.

She fell on her knees beside him, too grieved even to cry out. Her arms cradled her child's limp form and she laid her face against his.

The sheriff pushed his way through the silent crowd and stood towering over the mother and child.

"What has happened here?"

A man's voice came from somewhere in the crowd. "That boy was killed, and the person who did it is not far from him."

At that the crowd took up the murmur. "To think that a mother would kill her own child! That's why she can't cry!"

The sheriff told his men to take Josina to jail.

They left her alone in a bare stone cell. After a time she came out of her daze and realized what had befallen her child —and her. She pushed her hair back from her forehead and wept. "My child is dead," she moaned, "and I am in prison.

Why has this happened to me?" She stretched out on the cold floor. But she could not sleep or rest. The night seemed never-ending.

Early the next morning the sheriff came with his men. He took her rudely by the arm. "Come along with us to the linden tree. The aldermen are waiting."

Josina stood up with an effort. Her steps faltered as she followed the men. When she saw the linden tree in the distance, she bent her head. Now she knew, now she really knew, what terrible crime she was to be accused of.

It was a beautiful summer day. There wasn't a cloud in the sky. Larks soared into the blue and the air was filled with their singing. The yellow grain lay in sheaves on the fields, and against the walls of the houses flowers bloomed in a riot of color.

The sheriff stood forth and presented his case. For the first time, Josina heard the name of her accuser. He was the man she had refused to marry—the most important man in the village. Who would ever believe her word against his?

The aldermen asked him to tell what he knew. He stepped forward, never looking at the widow, and said that he had seen the whole deed. Josina and her son, he told the aldermen, had gone for a walk early in the morning. He had followed them because he had felt, somehow, that the widow had an evil plan in mind. When they came to the river, she had looked around furtively, and he had hidden himself behind a tree. From his hiding place he had watched as she seized her son and threw him into the river.

The people heard his story with horror. Everyone was silent. It was all plain and clear: Josina had murdered her son. No one would take her part. Death called for death, they believed. No other punishment was possible.

The oldest alderman looked at her sternly.

"What do you have to say?" he asked her.

Josina could not answer.

His voice was loud and angry. "What have you to say for yourself? Or are you silent because you are guilty?"

At that Josina lifted her head. "I am not guilty! I am innocent!"

There was a quaver in her voice. The people turned to one another, nodding sagely. That proved how guilty she was!

The sheriff said, "Do you mean to say that your accuser lies? What reason would he have for lying? He is a rich man —you are a poor woman."

"I am innocent. That's all I know."

The sheriff said furiously, "You are talking to men, not children! Don't lie to us."

The oldest alderman asked once more, "Have you nothing else to say? Only that you are innocent?"

Josina smiled at him, and because she smiled, the people were convinced that she was making sport of them and of her judges. The oldest alderman motioned for the sheriff to speak. No one noticed that the widow's accuser moved back and lost himself in the crowd.

The sheriff spoke. "This woman is guilty. We hold her the more guilty because she denies her guilt. At first we were unwilling to believe it, but the way she has acted proves our case. There can be no doubt about it—she killed her child and threw him into the Jeker. Why did she do it? Because of poverty? There is no one in Canne who would not have helped her if she had come to him. Every door would have been opened to her if she had asked for work for herself or food for her child. Is there anyone here who is not convinced of her guilt? Who among us believes that any person in the world would bear false testimony against a poor widow? Yet I will believe in her innocence, if I am given a sign. Only then. And the sign? If it snows—if night falls instantly on this beautiful summer day—I will believe in the innocence of this woman. Otherwise not!"

The widow stood with drooping head. The people were silent, so silent that they could hear a bird hopping on the topmost branch of the linden tree. The sheriff looked about triumphantly, proud of his speech.

And then, suddenly, the blue sky was filled with clouds. They spread over the heavens and covered the sun. Night fell swiftly. The birds stopped singing. The flowers dried on their stalks. The fields were lost in darkness. The shocks of grain, and the distant hills and the little chapel were no longer visible. No one could see his neighbor. They all stood still in complete darkness, amazed and frightened.

At last a faint edge of light appeared on the horizon. Then it grew deeper and broader and rose into the sky. The sun shone again; the birds took up their singing. And now the people could see the hills again, and the little chapel, and the linden tree.

When they saw the linden tree, a sharp gasp went up from them. Its leaves were covered with snow, and its great trunk was white. On the ground around it, summer insects ran about, a caterpillar crawled over the brown earth, a grasshopper warmed itself in the sun. Beneath the tree and everywhere around it summer had returned. But the snow on the linden tree did not melt. In the midst of the warmth and color of summertime, the linden tree remained white, and its branches were bent under the weight of the snow.

The oldest alderman stood up. His voice trembled with emotion when he spoke. "A sign has been given to us. In the face of this miracle, let no man question the widow's innocence."

There was a long sigh from the people standing beyond the linden tree. Then they turned to find Josina's accuser. But he had gone. And no one ever saw him again.

❧ A Legend of Saint Nicholas ❦

Nicholas, the Bishop of Myra in Asia Minor, was known for his many deeds of kindness. He liked to ride about the town on his white horse, with his faithful servant, Black Piet, walking beside him, and give oranges and toys to the children he met on his way. He cared for the sick, and helped the poor and lonely. People began to speak of him as Saint Nicholas.

The good bishop was particularly fond of entertaining travelers who had been to other lands, and one day a returned voyager told him of Holland. "The cities are full of water-ways," he said, "and the houses have stepped roofs. The children wear wooden shoes, and have round, merry faces. There are windmills in the fields, and the ports are full of white-sailed ships."

"I should like to see that country," the bishop said. He clapped his hands to summon his servant. "Black Piet, we are going to Holland. I will take ship tomorrow."

The bishop had the hold of the vessel filled with oranges, and toys, and sugarplums. Of course, his white horse had to go, too. It was winter and the sea was stormy. The winds rose and the waves were so high that the ship listed dangerously.

"We are doomed!" the sailors cried.

Only the bishop was calm. "Fear not," he said. He fell to his knees and prayed, and suddenly the seas were smooth again.

It was the fifth of December when the ship reached the harbor of Amsterdam. As soon as he came ashore a crowd surrounded Bishop Nicholas. The people wanted to stroke his white horse which carried baskets on either side. They wanted to touch the bishop's handsome embroidered robes. They liked his kindly face under the tall miter. And they had never seen anyone like Black Piet.

The children ran beside the bishop as he rode to the market square. There he distributed the good things that filled the baskets. The children clamored for the gifts. But first Bishop Nicholas would say to each one, "Have you been a good child this past year?" If the child said "Yes", he would ask the parents, "Has he truly been a good child this year?"

Those who had been good received the gifts, and those who had not been good found Black Piet shaking a switch at them, so that they ran and hid behind their mothers' skirts.

The crowd followed Bishop Nicholas around the city. "This is a beautiful country," he said. "I have always wanted to see it. And now that I have seen it, I know that I shall come back again."

The children brought sweet hay and carrots to feed the white horse. There was dancing and feasting and singing.

Somehow all the people know that this was a very special visitor, and they were happy to have him in their city. At the end of the day the children of Amsterdam fell asleep, their wooden shoes full of gifts.

As Bishop Nicholas and Black Piet wandered through the quiet streets, they heard the sound of weeping coming from a handsome house. The bishop got off his horse and went close to the house, to listen. "There are two sisters there," he whispered to Black Piet as he peered through one of the windows. "The room is empty. All the furniture is gone. Their eyes are red from weeping. Let us hear what they are saying."

The older sister said, "Where can we go? What can we do? The money our father left us is gone; we have sold all our belongings, we have nothing. Tomorrow we must leave this house, but where can we go?"

The younger sister said, "Do not despair. I will pray God to take care of us." They both bent their heads.

Bishop Nicholas and Black Piet crept away. Late that night, when the sisters were asleep on the bare floor, the bishop came back and silently put a big bag of gold through the window, where they would find it the first thing in the morning.

On the way back to his lodgings, the bishop passed a lowly hovel. He knew that the people in this little hut must be miserably poor, and he wanted to do something for them. But he could not put money through a window, for there were no windows in the hut. And the door was tightly closed against the cold.

The good bishop was puzzled. "How can I get inside to leave money for them?"

Black Piet pointed to the sloping thatched roof. "Why not climb up to the chimney?" And that is what Bishop Nicholas did. Carefully he dropped a handful of gold coins down the chimney, and by a miracle they fell into the stockings which

the two children of the household had hung in the fireplace to dry.

Next morning, when they found the coins, the children could not believe their eyes. "It's a gift direct from the good God!" they cried.

But a neighbor, who had seen the bishop clambering over the roof, told them what had happened.

Although everyone hunted over the city for the bringer of gifts and Black Piet, they had disappeared and their ship was gone from the harbor.

But the next year Bishop Nicholas came back, and every year since then he has returned, to bring gifts to the children of Holland on the night of December fifth. When he died, he was made a saint, and the day of his visitation is called Sinterklaas, which is Saint Nicholas in Dutch, and from this we get our Santa Claus.

The beloved bishop became the patron saint of sailors and of the city of Amsterdam; the largest church there is named in his honor. Cakes are made in his image and sold in the streets.

Every year Saint Nicholas visits all the homes in Holland, rich and poor. On the night of December fifth, the children put their wooden shoes in the chimney corner, filled with carrots or hay for his white horse.

❧ Emma of Haarlem ❦

ONCE UPON A TIME, a wicked knight lived in the castle of Haarlem. Though he was hated by his people, whom he oppressed cruelly, he was loved by his wife, for he was a kind and thoughtful husband.

Emma of Haarlem knew that her husband was abhorred by his subjects. Though she begged him to be merciful to them, he rode over his serfs' newly planted fields, not caring that their crops would be ruined. When a peasant died, the knight would take the best of his cattle, and even the iron pots from the dead man's house, leaving little for the widow and children. He made the men work for him when the weather was fine, and would let them tend their own fields only when he could not use them.

71

When his serfs met him, they kept their eyes on the ground lest he see the hatred in them. The knight would smile to himself as he looked at their averted faces and bent backs.

Distrust and fury smouldered in the peasants' hearts, though the lord of the castle did not know it. At last, the serfs realized that he would never change. They took up arms and marched on the castle.

Before the knight knew what had happened, they had surrounded it. No messenger could be sent to ride for help. Now the knight was afraid of his aroused people.

He had never thought that his castle would be encircled. Why hadn't he thought to lay in enough food to last during a siege? He knew that even if his garrison could get out and kill a great number of the peasants, there would be others to take their places.

Food grew scarce in the castle, and finally there was none. The angry peasants knew well that hunger was their ally. They would starve their lord into submission.

"We will have to surrender," the knight said at last. "We can't defend ourselves against famine."

Emma, his wife, said, "Don't be afraid. I will save your life."

"How can you?"

She smiled at him. "Let me go and talk to the people."

"It will do no good," the knight said gloomily. "What can a *woman* do that men can't do?"

"Let me try," she begged.

He agreed, and she went out on the ramparts to speak to the people who were besieging the castle. They listened while she spoke to them. They had no wish to harm *her*. It was her husband they hated.

"What it it you want?" they asked her.

Emma said, "I want you to let me and my serving-women leave the castle."

They were not concerned with the lady and her serving-women. *They* could do no harm, and there was no reason why they should not leave the castle. The peasants were storing their wrath against the day when they could take the knight himself. They agreed that Emma and her serving-women might leave the castle.

She thanked them. "But," she asked sadly, "must I go through the country poor and shabby? Is nothing of my wealth to be left to me?"

"We are not fighting for your wealth," they told her. "What do you want to take with you?"

"Let me, I beseech you, take my most precious possession."

"Granted."

She hesitated, and they asked her what else she desired.

"Will you give me your word," Emma asked, "that I can

go safely past you when I carry out my most precious possession? Swear to me that you will not touch my treasure."

They all swore that she would not be harmed when she carried her most precious possession from the castle. They wanted to show her that they craved only their freedom, not her riches.

Emma thanked them again, and returned to the castle. She ran happily to her husband. "We are saved!" she cried.

She put him on her back. Bent double under his weight, she went out of the castle and across the drawbridge. With slow, painful steps she staggered between the rows of silent people who had given their word that they would not touch her treasure. They kept their word. They clutched their weapons and clenched their fists as they remembered the deeds of the wicked knight but they let Emma of Haarlem pass, carrying her dearest possession.

Only when she was far beyond the last man did she set her burden down. Then Emma and the knight looked behind them. A cloud of smoke, like a mist, hung over the castle, and while they watched, a tongue of flame shot from the tower.

⪫ The Cat-Chalice of Vlaardingen ⪪

EARLY ONE MORNING, before the sun was fairly up, two boys stood on the sea-dike at Vlaardingen. The day looked like any other day. They shivered. It was still cold.

"Look, a ship!" one of them called suddenly to the other.

"Where, where? You're dreaming!"

"One—two—three masts."

"I don't see anything."

"Are you blind?" The boy pointed excitedly.

Out of the mist, in the dim light of dawn, a three-masted ship was gliding noiselessly toward them. It was like a ship in a dream. The two boys were curious, although they didn't know why. They had certainly seen plenty of ships. This ship came slowly, slowly, through the mist, and dawn had turned into day before it finally anchored in the harbor. The two boys still stood there, lost in wonder.

"There are almost no men on board," one of them said. "Did you notice? Only women."

"Yes, and they're dressed in sailcloth."

"The one at the helm is certainly a man. Brr, what long whiskers he has!"

"His eyes are so strange. See how he's looking at us."

"The women aren't doing anything but talking. Nobody on board seems to be working."

"How high the ship rides! I wonder if she has any cargo."

"Look how the women are pushing one another, trying to get ashore! Isn't anyone going to stay on the ship?"

By this time fishermen, and carpenters, and sailmakers, and ropemakers, and tradesmen were coming to the sea-dike. They asked each other, "What kind of ship is this?" And they said, puzzled, "We've never seen a ship like this in the harbor of Vlaardingen."

And yet, when it came down to it, no one could say exactly why this ship seemed different from other vessels. What they really meant was that this was the kind of ship one sees in a dream.

Helmsman and sailors sprang onto the wall. And as soon as their feet touched the ground, they turned into cats, slim, lithe, and miaowing. The helmsman became a big, fat tomcat with round, fierce green eyes. The people of Vlaardingen were frightened, and fled—street urchins and tradesmen alike.

The cats, led by the strutting tomcat, followed one another in a long line through the streets of the town. "Sss-miaaw-mioo," the leader said. And suddenly the cats stopped where they were.

One cat, young and agile, ran back the way they had come, toward the harbor. It dragged a tiny ship made of a nutshell

from the water. The masts were three pins with little pieces of cloth for sails, and the wheel was a pinhead. The cat dug in the ground with its little paws, flinging the sand carelessly to one side. It dropped the nutshell into the hole and pushed the sand over it hastily. "Miaow!" And the cat ran back to its comrades. As soon as the nutshell was buried, the big ship in the harbor disappeared.

The cats' wild march began again. No street was left unvisited. The big tomcat led the mad rush; the little cats had a hard time keeping up with him. At last, he halted and ordered all the cats to form a circle around him. Between his forepaws he held a silver beaker and, while they watched, he lifted it and drank from it greedily. Then he passed the beaker to a beautiful cat, his belovéd. "Miaow-mi-o-o."

The beautiful cat drank from the chalice, and then gave it to her best friend, with whom she had danced paw-to-paw. "Mia-mia," she said softly.

Just then a kitten, her back arched, sprang forward and grabbed the beaker from the paws of the cat that held it. "Yaapsg!" she spat, and pressed her claws against the side of the silver cup, holding it fast. She stared defiantly up into the eyes of the tomcat and lifted the beaker to her mouth, drinking with quick little licks of her tongue. All of her friends and enemies crowded around, demanding a drink from the chalice, too, and when they had drunk from it, danced madly down the road—singly and in pairs.

A wagon can along the road. It was loaded with garden produce and two farmers sat on the high seat beside the driver. The cats heard the rumble of the wheels, and stopped their dance. They waited motionless in the road.

The wagon drew nearer. The driver whipped up his horses, for he and the other farmers were in a hurry to get to the market at Delft.

"Giddap, you lazy nags!" he shouted to the horses. Their hoofs struck sparks from the stones. "Giddap!"

The cats went to stand in front of the oncoming wagon. The horses reared on their hind legs; their eyes were wild with fright.

"Out of the way, beasts!" the driver cried.

But the cats, with the tomcat in the lead, swayed to right and left. They danced crazily across the road and up and down it, paw linked to paw. The two horses could not move. Their coats were wet with sweat.

"Let us pass!" the driver demanded furiously.

"We will let you pass," the tomcat said merrily, "after you have drunk to my belovéd, the great Cypress-cat Marioma, who is here beside me. No poet can begin to sing the praises of my lovely Cypress-cat Marioma; there is no more beautiful creature in the world than she!"

"Pres-sssssss!" the kitten hissed jealously, but the tomcat ignored her.

He said to the angry driver, "I want you to do Marioma honor by drinking to her from this beaker!"

"Never!" said the driver. "Never!" He slashed the whip through the air. "Giddap!"

"Mia-o-mia-o," sang the cats. They danced in wild rows before the horses.

> Drink, drink to my beautiful one!
> You'll never go till that you've done!

The tomcat sang and all the other cats joined in—except the kitten.

"Nay, that I will not do! Not even for the Devil," the driver yelled.

The cats surrounded the wagon; they drew closer to one another until they had made a tight ring around it. The tom-cat laughed.

"Then you'll never get through, driver," he sneered. "You'll never make it to Delft. Your vegetables will rot in the wagon. You'll never sell your butter and eggs."

The other farmers were worried. They began to mutter to each other. If they did not get to market, they would lose money. They did not see why they should be held up by these crazy dancing cats and the stubborn driver. They poked him in the ribs.

"Go ahead. Do it. We've got to get to market. Go ahead. Drink."

The driver said slowly, "Very well. But in God's name only." And he stretched forth his hand for the chalice.

Now no sooner had he said those last five words than the ring of cats broke up, and they began to rush helter-skelter, pell-mell toward the sea-dike. They didn't stop to think about the order of their going. In fact, the mighty tomcat was running faster then any of them.

The first cat to reach the shore dug frantically where the nutshell was buried. Its sharp claws made the sand fly. Two other cats grasped the nutshell in their paws, holding it fast. They rolled it before them to the water and threw it in. It sank, but rose again, and when it rose, the pinhead was a steering wheel, the nutshell a ship, the pins were masts with strong white sails. The cats sprang on board, and as soon as their paws touched the deck they were women again, dressed in sailcloth. The big tomcat became a bewhiskered, fat helmsman in a red flannel shirt. The sails filled with the wind, and the ship began to move. It rode out to sea, and disappeared.

The silver beaker still lay where the cats had dropped it. A trickle of red wine flowed over the stones in the road.

It was very quiet in the town of Vlaardingen.

✍ The Haunted House ✍

Not so long a haunted house stood near Dokkum. Every night, on the stroke of twelve, there was a most terrible noise in one of its bedrooms. No one would sleep in that room, and all the furniture had been removed from it except an old bed.

The people who lived in the house had tried to find out what caused this unearthly noise but, since no one was brave enough to stay in the room at night, it remained a mystery.

One evening, when it had been raining for a week, a little old woman came to the door. The trees were dripping, the streets were flooded, water ran in a swift stream down the road. The leaden skies seemed to have endless rain left in them. The fields had begun to look like lakes, and it was difficult to get about.

The poor woman was soaked to the skin. Rain dripped from her hair onto her shoulders. Her shoes squished with water. She had tried to put her skirt over her head as a kind of umbrella, but that was soaked, too.

She was timid about knocking on the door, but she thought, "The people who live here can only tell me to go away—that's the worst they can do."

But to her amazement the maid who answered the door asked the old woman to step inside. A couple of children peered curiously at her from the other end of the hall. She beckoned to them to come nearer, for she loved children, but they turned and ran away.

An old gentleman came out of the dining room. "Would you like to spend the night here, little lady?" he asked.

"Oh, yes, please, mijnheer."

"And you're not afraid?"

"Why should I be afraid?"

"Would you dare to sleep in a haunted room? It's the only one that isn't occupied."

"In any room, mijnheer, even if there were a dozen ghosts."

He looked at her sharply. "Well, come along with me."

As she walked beside him, the little old woman looked back and saw the trail of water she was leaving. "It's a pity to drip over your nice floor," she apologized.

"Think nothing of it," he said. "If you are willing to spend the night in the haunted room, I'll be most grateful. Then, perhaps, we'll come to the end of this mystery."

There was nothing special about the room, except that it was furnished only with the old bed. The walls were thick, and the sill under the one window was wide. The old gentleman sat down on it, and looked at his guest thoughtfully.

"Are you sure you're not afraid?"

"If mijnheer had been walking in the rain as long as I have

been, he wouldn't be afraid, either. I am far too tired to be afraid." She watched the water dripping from her clothing onto the floor.

He said, "I suppose you'd like to go right to bed?"

"If mijnheer would send me a towel so that I can dry myself, I will be grateful. Then I shall go to sleep in that beautiful bed."

"*One* towel!" cried the old gentleman. "I'll have them bring you ten!"

When she had dried herself, the old woman climbed into the bed, and fell asleep at once, despite the sound of the rain pounding on the roof. She slept right around the clock. And when she woke in the early morning, the door was opening slowly, and a little girl was peering around it.

"Come in, little one!"

"Are you the rain-lady?"

"Why, what a nice name you've thought up for me! And what's your name, my dear?"

"Annetje."

"And how old are you?"

"Four, and next week I have a birthday." The little girl looked at the rain-lady. "Why aren't you dripping any more?"

"I slept between dry sheets, and I don't want even to think about rain!"

They heard a loud voice in the hall. Annetje looked frightened. "Oh, that's Grandfather. He said that I must never come into this room."

The old woman had forgotten all about the ghost; she decided that she had better go at once. She dressed hastily and slipped quietly down the stairs. As she was opening the outer door, she remembered that she had not thanked her host for his kindness.

When she found him, he shook his head. "Do you mean

you would have gone away without telling me what happened in that room during the night?"

"Happened?" she said. "Nothing happened. I slept."

"Didn't the ghost appear? Why, in *my* room, I heard that horrible racket at midnight!"

The woman said, "Would you like me to stay in the haunted room another night? This time I'll try to keep awake to see if the ghost comes."

"That would be fine." He called one of the maids. "See that our guest has everything she wants."

That night the old woman went to bed early to that she could get her sleep before midnight. Suddenly she awoke, and sat up in bed. It was pitch-dark outside, but in the room there was a dim blue light. Where did it come from? Should she call her host?

Near the window a figure was walking back and forth. She could hear the footsteps, as measured as those of a sentry. But she felt no fear. Peering out between the bed curtains, she called, "Who are you?"

The ghost came toward her, and held his hand in front of her face. "Go back to sleep!" he ordered.

The old woman sighed and settled her nightcap on her head. "Well, if you say so, I'll go back to sleep. But hurry up with whatever you're doing, will you?"

"Hmmm," the ghost said. "You don't seem to be afraid of me."

She lay down again, and pretended to sleep. But she kept her eyes half-open, and whenever the ghost looked toward her, she almost closed them. She could see him well enough between her narrowed lids. He was tall and thin, and wore a dirty cap on his sparse hair and dilapidated slippers on his feet. His trousers were ragged and there were big slits in his coat; there was a sprinkling of dust on his shoulders.

All at once, with frightening speed, he leaped onto the wide window sill. He dug his fingernails into the wood and lay there, howling. The rain-lady sat up again, but a little more cautiously than the first time.

With one bound, the ghost sprang toward the bed, and she barely had time to throw herself down again, pretending to snore, before she felt his eyes boring into her. He shook his fist at her, and his fingers rattled like dry bones.

Now the old woman was really frightened. She could almost feel his hands around her throat, and she heard his voice in her ear, saying "Lie still, and see nothing!"

As soon as he turned back to the window, she raised herself on one elbow and parted the bed curtains. She saw the ghost take some carpenter's tools from his pocket—a hammer, a file, a small saw. He began to work on the window sill, ripping out the woodwork below it.

Just as he tore the last board loose, a torrent of golden ducats poured onto the floor in a clinking stream. The ghost squatted and pulled more coins, of gold and silver, from a hollow place in the wall. Then he began to put the coins in piles, counting, counting, in a hoarse voice.

The little old woman hardly dared breathe, but she soon saw that his mind was only on the money. Suddenly the clock in the hall began to strike. The ghost leaped up, flung the coins back, helter-skelter, into the hole beneath the window sill, replaced the boards, and on the last stroke of midnight, he disappeared into thin air.

The woman wondered if she had dreamed what she had seen. She lay wide-awake, listening to the rain which was still falling from the dark skies, and waited for morning. As soon as it was light, she dressed and crept down the stairs. A sleepy maidservant met her in the hall.

"Was the ghost there?" the girl asked.

"Yes. Tell your master to get up. There is a fortune in that room."

Soon all the family had gathered around her. "Tell us what happened," they cried. But when she told them, they could not believe it.

"Go and look," she urged. "You will find riches there you never dreamed of."

Even so, they would not take her word for it until they had pried up the window sill. Then a great gasp went up, for the money fell out in a seemingly endless stream. It covered the floor.

When the stream of coins finally stopped, the old woman said, "But where did all these coins come from? How did they get here?"

The grandfather was the only one who could answer her. He said, "In this house, long ago, there lived a miser. His neighbors did not know much about him, but they did know that he was a mean and selfish man. He drove the poor from his door rather than give them a crust. One time he even sold the home of one of his debtors just because he wanted more money.

"When he died there was no one to mourn him. Not a penny was found in the house, so he was buried in a pauper's grave. People wondered what had happened to all the money he must have had. In the great carved chests they found only cast-off clothing.

"No one ever thought of this hiding place. Who would have imagined that money would be hidden under a window sill? That was probably why the miser's ghost came back to this room every night. His punishment must have been to count the coins over and over again, as he had done in his lifetime, until, by some chance, they were found by living people.

"Now," the old gentleman concluded, "I am sure he will never come back."

"Do you really think so?" the little old woman said. "Then I am glad that I was able to lay the ghost."

"Yes," he said, "and for that reason, and to show our gratitude, I invite you to stay with us always."

She shook her head. "What would I do here? No, I must go as I came." She pulled her skirt over her head again and, without another word, went out into the rain.

The rain poured off the roof and the wind drove it in gusts down the road. The children ran to the door, calling after the woman, "Come back, rain-lady! Come back!" But she did not seem to hear them, and disappeared into the mists.

≥ Why Pigs Root ≤

HAVE YOU EVER NOTICED how pigs root along the ground, as if they were hunting for something? There's a reason for this.

One day a farmer found that his wife's pancake pan was very rusty. He tried to polish it, but the rust wouldn't come off. In disgust, he went to the market and bought a new pan. This one was bright and smooth; it sparkled in the sunlight. There wasn't a spot on it.

As he approached his house, the farmer was very hungry. He would give the new pan to his wife and ask her to make some pancakes for him right away. But his wife had gone to visit a neighbor.

"Why should I wait until she comes back?" the farmer

said to himself. "When she does, she may not feel like making pancakes. I may as well make them myself."

He took a stick and poked up the fire. Then he beat up the batter, all the while growing more and more hungry. When a man is hungry, there is nothing like a thin, lucious pancake, hot from the pan and covered with sugar! He poured some batter into the pan and sniffed the air as the pancake began to brown. Now was the time to turn it.

But that wasn't so easy. The farmer had never made pancakes before and didn't know how to flip the pan. The pancake fell on the floor. And the door was open.

"Aha!" the pancake cried. "This is the chance of a lifetime! I've always wanted to see the world."

The pancake rolled out of the door, before the farmer could blink. It rolled along the path and onto the road.

After a little while it came to a rabbit. "Good morning!" said the rabbit.

"Good morning to you!" answered the pancake.

"How about my eating you?" the rabbit asked eagerly.

"Mercy, no!" the pancake said. "The very idea! I'll say good day." And with that, it went on its way, much faster than the rabbit could run.

A short distance farther it came to a fox. "Good morning," said the fox, with a friendly smile.

"Good morning!" the pancake answered.

"Shall we walk along together a bit?" the fox inquired, coming closer.

"Not for all the money in the world!" the pancake answered hurriedly. "One is better than two. However, all good wishes!"

And with that the pancake rolled along, faster and faster, until everyone who saw it had pinwheels before his eyes.

Suddenly it came to a great, fat pig lying in the road. "Good morning!" he grunted.

"Good morning to you," the pancake answered in a light, high voice.

"What did you say?" the pig inquired.

"I said, Good morning," the pancake repeated.

"I can't hear you," the pig said. "I'm a little deaf. Ever since my birth, I've been deaf in one ear. Won't you come around to the other side?"

"Why, of course," the pancake answered, and it rolled around to the other side of the pig.

Just as it was about to say, "Good morning," once again, the pig's mouth snapped open and he grabbed the pancake.

But his mouth couldn't open wide enough to grab the *whole* pancake—he could swallow only half of it.

The other half curled itself up and rolled into the ground— deeper, deeper, and deeper.

The pig thought the half of the pancake he had eaten was so delicious that he simply must have the rest. He began to search for the missing half. With his snout, he rooted in the earth, hunting, hunting, hunting.

And so, as I said, whenever you see a pig rooting in the earth, snuffling and searching all over, you will know why. He is hunting for the other half of that delectable pancake.

⪢ The Miserly Miller ⪡

MORE THAN SEVEN HUNDRED YEARS AGO the devout scholar
Oliverus of Cologne traveled along the river Maas in Holland,
stopping in each town and village. He gathered the people
around him and told them that Jerusalem, the burial place of
Christ, was in the hands of infidels. An army of Christians was
going to the Holy Land, to wrest it from the Saracens, the un-
believers.

There was hardly a woman who heard Oliverus who did not
long to do something for him. Every young lad could feel a
sword in his hand and was on fire to be part of the great army
that would free the Holy Land. There was not an oldster who
did not yearn to be young again.

When Oliverus spoke in Maastricht, there was a miser who

stood in the midst of the crowd and thought to himself, "No one need wait for *me* to join these young fools! They'll ask me for money, no doubt. They think I'm rich, and that I will give them a hundred silver marks. Just because I'm the owner of the Black Mill they think they'll get a hundred marks. Well, as surely as my name is Godelas, they're wrong! They'll be lucky to get five!"

The people along the Maas who had heard Oliverus speak could not forget him. His voice, his words, stayed with them. Women gave their last pennies to help swell the fund that the Christians needed for the long voyage to the Holy Land. Men and boys, young and old, joined the army in a fever to fight the Saracens.

They asked Godelas to give money. "Give with full hands," they begged. "You're old, Godelas; Heaven or Hell isn't far from you."

"Give, give!" he cried angrily. "That's all I hear. 'Give to me,' a child says. 'Give to me,' says a young boy. 'Give to me,' says a man. Everybody wants to pluck money from one who has it. Listen! I saw a tree one time, full of green leaves, and a few weeks later there wasn't one on it, because caterpillars had crawled along the branches and nibbled every leaf. Go to my neighbor's house—he's rich enough to give you plenty!"

"Didn't you hear what Oliverus said?"

"Oh, Oliverus! Who cares what he said? Are we in such a state that we need to have a stranger come here and tell us what to do and what to think and what to give? However, I won't let you go away without something. You can't spread the tale that I'm miserly."

"You are rich, Godelas, we all know that," the people told him. "It wouldn't hurt you to give us a hundred marks. You wouldn't even miss them."

"Ho-ho!" he laughed mirthlessly. "I've heard that little song before! How can you measure my wealth? Anyone can tell how deep the water is in a pot or how wide a field is, or how heavy a sack of flour is. But no one can know how much money another man has."

"Do you mean," the men said in amazemennt, "that you refuse to give any money at all?"

"No, I'm not refusing to give *any* money. I give from my poverty," he said, and slapped five silver marks on the table. His visitors gazed at them, and at him, and then, without saying a word of thanks, they got up and left. When Godelas was alone, he burst out laughing. "The simpletons!" he said.

For he really thought they were simpletons, or worse, to give up their lives, or their wealth, just to win the Holy Land back from the Saracens.

One day some of the crusaders went past his house on their way to the Holy Land. They marched proudly, thinking of the words of Oliverus. Godelas stood in his doorway and mocked them.

"How many of you, do you think, will come back? Why in the world are you going out there to die?"

No one answered him.

"I bought myself off for five silver marks. Do you know what each of you is actually worth? Just five silver marks, you fools!"

They did not even turn their heads. The miller went into his house.

It was summer, and the stream on which his mill stood was sandy and quiet. The big wheels of the mill had no power behind them; that must wait till the stream was full and fast-flowing again. In the middle of the night Godelas woke up, wondering what he had heard. It must have been a dream, he thought, but it sounded exactly as if the big wheels of the mill were turning.

Maybe it was the wind blowing through the trees. No, that wasn't it. He knew that sound all too well—it *was* the wheels of his mill! And the mill had been silent for days because of the lack of water.

The noise grew louder. The wheels seemed to rattle and roar; his whole house shook with the noise. The miller became very angry. What scoundrel was in there, running his mill? If he caught the vandal he would tear him limb from limb.

He called his servant. "Go and see what's happening, and report to me at once! Someone's grinding meal—I can hear the millstones turning."

Godelas waited and listened. He heard the water in the stream, roaring and foaming as if it were coming from a mountainside in the middle of winter.

"Why doesn't that wretch of a Jan come back?" he fumed, holding his ears against the noise.

Just then he heard the man's footsteps. They were slow and dragging—like a prisoner's. Jan came in and stood there, his head bowed.

"Well? Speak up! What's going on in the mill?"

Jan couldn't answer. He stretched out his arms. He was too frightened to speak. Together they stood listening to the unholy racket of the mill, the hissing and foaming of the angry brook.

"You dolt! If you can't speak, I'll go and see for myself!" Godelas shouted. He pulled on his clothes and rushed out. When he opened the door of the mill, he could hardly see. But finally he made out a figure in a black cloak, standing near the grinding stones. He moved closer. The miller saw, with horror, what was being ground relentlessly under the heavy stones—five silver marks.

Now the dark figure spoke. "I have two horses, Godelas. Come with me."

The miller felt as if this was a nightmare. It was the Devil himself who had come for him. He reached out and swept Godelas up as easily as if he had been a child. He carried him out to the waiting horses and flung him over the nearer one. "We are going for a long ride, Godelas," he said.

Then he mounted his own horse, and wrapped his black cloak closer about him. The sound of the grinding millstones followed them into the night. And no one ever heard of Godelas again.

⊰ The Poffertjes Pan ⊱

JAN THE SHOEMAKER, and Katrina his wife lived happily together until one snowy winter evening. Then Katrina said, "Wouldn't it be nice to have some poffertjes?" (Poffertjes are little, fat, hot cakes, covered with sugar.) "The only trouble is I can't find my poffertjes pan."

Jan said, "Then we can't have poffertjes."

His wife replied, "Now, don't be silly. Mevrouw Smid has one. Run over and ask her if we may borrow it."

"But I have work to do. The burgomeester's shoes aren't ready."

"Do you or don't you want poffertjes? *My* mouth is watering for them!"

The shoemaker got up with a sigh and hung his leather

apron on a peg. "Tell Mevrouw Smid," said Katrina, "that if she will let us have her pan, I will make the best poffertjes she ever ate and I will send her some for her kindness."

When Jan returned, his wife had the batter all ready, and soon the little room was filled with the appetizing aroma of poffertjes browning in their pan. When she flipped them out onto the platter and dusted them with sugar they looked so good that first Jan, and then Katrina, began sampling them one by one. In no time at all, there wasn't a single poffertje left.

"Oh, my goodness," said Katrina. "I completely forgot to save some for Mevrouw Smid. You will have to take the pan back to her, Jan, without them."

"I'll do no such thing. Take it back to her yourself! You were the one who promised her the poffertjes. I have my work to do."

"You borrowed the pan, so you must take it back," she insisted.

"Be quiet, woman! I must get the burgomeester's shoes ready." He sat down at his bench and took up his awl.

Katrina put her hands on her hips. "Very well! I'll *be* quiet! You'll not hear another word out of me. The first one of us to speak will have to take the pan back."

The shoemaker did not answer. He just nodded his head, and smiled to himself. *He* wouldn't be the first one to speak. Try as she might, his wife wouldn't get a word out of *him!*

For a long while there was quiet in the little room, except for the whirr of Katrina's spinning wheel, and the thump-thump of Jan's mallet on the last. Then the door opened and Kees, the burgomeester's servant, came in rubbing his cold hands.

"I've come for mijnheer's shoes. Are they ready?"

The shoemaker looked up, but said nothing.

"Well, answer me! Are they ready?"

Still the shoemaker said nothing. The servant turned to Katrina. "What's the matter with your husband? Is he deaf?"

She barely glanced at him, and went on with her spinning. Kees cried angrily, "Have you both lost your tongues? What's the matter with you?" But neither one spoke. At that, the servant rushed out of the room, slamming the door behind him.

He went back to the burgomeester's house. "The shoemaker and his wife have both gone mad," he said. "I can't get a word out of either of them."

"Then you didn't bring my shoes? I'll see about this. Come along with me."

The two of them marched to the shoemaker's house. The burgomeester entered without knocking and strode up to Jan. "What does this mean? You were to have my shoes ready, and Kees says he can't get a word out of you."

Jan clamped his lips shut. The burgomeester's face grew red. He grabbed Jan by the ear. "Answer me, stupid one! If you won't speak, and if you don't give my my shoes, I'll take everything you have in payment. Kees, take that cloth from the table, and pack up whatever you can carry in it."

While the servant went around the room, gathering up the pewter plates and the brass candlestick and the good china bowl, Jan had all he could do to restrain himself. Katrina started up from her spinning wheel, and held out her hands as if to stop Kees. Then she sank back again upon her stool, and hid her eyes. When the man picked up Katrina's best lace cap, Jan thought surely his wife would cry out, but not a sound came from her.

Then Kees, wandering around the room, saw Jan's favorite long-stemmed clay pipe, lying on the mantlepiece. Jan leaped up from his bench. That pipe meant more to him than anything in the world. When he was a young man, he had skated all the way to Gouda for it—twelve miles. After he bought it, he had skated all the way home, with the pipe fastened to the top of his cap to prove that he had not fallen once on the long trip.

"Don't take that! You can't take that!" he shouted.

Katrina sprang to her feet, pointing her finger at him, and laughing. "You spoke first, Jan! Now, go at once, and take back Mevrouw Smid's poffertjes pan."

⋟ *Jan the Eighth Van Arkel* ⋞

THE BURGHERS OF GORINCHEM were rebelling against their count, Jan VIII Van Arkel. His men were worried, but the count only laughed.

"What if they rise up and besiege your castle?" the men asked.

"Those burghers are common folk, lowborn and close to the earth. They'll drop their weapons as soon as they see me," Jan answered.

The count knew very well that his followers didn't believe him. How could anyone else know what confidence he had in himself?

"You'll never see the burghers of Gorinchem here," he said. "But I will go to them. I'll show them how powerful I am!"

As soon as the sun was up the next morning, he started on his way. The early light glittered on his armor. He rode directly to the gates of Gorinchem.

The burghers were astonished at his courage, for he rode alone. Suddenly they were afraid of a trap. Were his soldiers perhaps following him at a distance? They looked down the road, but could see no sign of them. Proudly Jan Van Arkel rode through the gates, putting himself into the burghers' power. The people milled around him, marveling at his courage. This sort of thing had never happend before. They began to mutter together.

"Shouldn't we take him prisoner?"

"Should we kill him?"

"Doesn't he know how discontented we are? How can we force him to listen to our complaints?"

They growled and argued among themselves.

Jan Van Arkel smiled to himself. He looked more like a noble who was visiting his loyal people than a man whose life might hang on a single word. He acted as if he didn't notice the somber, angry faces around him as he stroked his horse's neck.

The horse stood quietly under his hand. The crowd saw that Jan Van Arkel was looking up. A wooden beam projecting from one of the house walls was directly over his head. He stretched his arms, and his hands grasped the wood. Everyone watched, wondering what was about to happen.

The count lifted himself up a bit, his knees still pressing hard against the flanks of his horse. Then he tightened his grip, and he and his horse rose as one in the air, so that the hoofs of the animal dangled far above the ground. Its eyes were starting from its head and its tongue hung out, so terrible was the pressure of the count's knees on its sides.

After a moment, Jan Van Arkel let himself and his steed

sink down slowly again. The horse stood still, breathing hard. Jan Van Arkel said not a word, but stared straight ahead into the distance.

The burghers stood rooted to the ground. Who could think of resisting a ruler like this? The men bowed their heads as a sign of their submission, and the women knelt.

Jan VIII Van Arkel rode out of the city as proudly as a victorious general. He had suppressed the rebellion of the burghers of Gorinchem with his two bare hands.

❧ The Knight of Steenhuisheerd ❦

IN THE NORTHERN PART OF HOLLAND there was once a large
castle called Steenhuisheerd. In it lived a knight who was tall
and handsome, but quick-tempered, and so proud that he felt
the world belonged to him. When he fell in love with a beautiful and noble maiden, he was sure that she would accept his
offer of marriage at once.

But she said, "I will marry you when you have overcome
your greatest enemy."

"That I can do. I am a mighty warrior."

She asked gently, "Do you know who this enemy is?"

He lifted his head quickly. "I will find him."

Her voice was firm but a little sad as she said, "Don't expect
to hear his name from me, if you cannot find him yourself."

The knight was not disturbed. Leaping onto his horse, he turned to say, "Wait just a few days, my lovely one, and you will hear his name from *me!*"

Now the knight had many enemies because of his pride and quick temper. He had even killed a man in anger one time. While he rode along the highway, he tried to think who his greatest enemy was, and he decided it was probably another knight whose brother he had defeated in battle. He had heard, any number of times, that this man was bent on revenge.

"I will go to his castle," he thought; but suddenly he reined in his horse. What good would it do him to kill this man? *His* nearest relative would vow revenge. He could almost hear his belovéd saying, "Now you have made another enemy."

He turned his horse around and rode slowly back to his castle, wondering all the while *who* could be his greatest enemy?

It puzzled him all night, and he turned the question over and over in his mind. In the morning he was no nearer an answer. There was no use asking his belovéd to tell him, for she had said she would not. And if he went to her again, she would think it was just an excuse to be near her. Besides, it would be a blow to his pride to ask her for the name, for hadn't he said that he would find his greatest enemy?

For ten days the knight stayed away from the maiden's home. At last he could stand it no longer and went to see her. "You must tell me whom you mean!" he demanded. "Man or devil, I'll overpower him."

She gazed at him thoughtfully. "It is neither man nor devil. It is your own hasty temper. That is your greatest enemy."

He cried, "But how can I overcome it?"

"Go to church," she told him, "and listen humbly to the Mass. Pray God to help you."

He bent his proud head. He had never dreamed that this

would be her answer. "Very well," he said, "I will do it—because you ask it."

She held out her hands to him. "And when you have overcome your enemy, I will be waiting for you."

The very next day, the knight decided to go to a chapel on the other side of the forest, and he started early. He would conquer his hasty temper if that was what he had to do, and the sooner the better. In a fever of impatience, he took the shortest way, which led him through the woods. Almost at once he glimpsed a stag through the trees, and he set off in pursuit of it. It was a beautiful creature, with the most handsome antlers he had ever seen, and he was determined to have them to hang upon the wall of the great hall in his castle.

After a long chase, they came to a brook. The stag swam across and fled over the swampy ground beyond. The knight urged his horse through the water, but when they came to the far bank, the horse floundered through the bog, and the knight soon lost the stag's trail.

His temper rose and he whipped his tired horse across the brook again and through the forest to the little church. As he approached it, he saw people streaming out of the doors. The service was over. The priest stood alone on the porch, and watched the knight ride up.

"Say the Mass again!" the knight commanded.

The priest said gently, "You forget yourself, my son. How can you ask a thing like that of me?"

The knight lifted his sword with a threatening gesture. "I will kill you if you don't do as I say."

The priest stood still. "My life is in your hands. But not my will. I do not fear death."

It seemed to the knight of Steenhuisheerd that a red mist swam in front of his eyes. When his sight cleared, he saw the priest lying on the ground, motionless, and he saw the bloody sword in his own hand.

He sprang onto his horse and rode like one pursued to the castle of his belovéd. She was waiting for him.

"Did you hear the Mass?" she asked him, smiling.

His answer was short. "No."

Slowly her smile faded. "Then you didn't do what I asked you to do?"

He said, in a muffled voice, "I came too late."

She looked at the sheath of his sword. There was a red stain upon it. "Whom have you killed now?"

He answered angrily, "The priest."

She was horror-stricken. "How could you do a thing like that?"

The knight bit his lip. "He wouldn't say the Mass a second time."

Her face was pale. She pointed to the door. "Go," she ordered. "I could never love you now. Forget that you ever loved me!"

"No one," he pleaded, "could ever love you more than I do. Whatever you ask of me, I will do."

She said sternly, "You need not hope that I will ever relent. I regret the day I first met you." Without another word, she turned and left him.

Furious, and with no sign of repentance, the knight rushed from the hall and vaulted upon his horse. He yanked viciously at the reins. The priest had not obeyed him—*that* was why he had had to die! Everyone was his enemy! No one cared for him!

As he drew near to his own castle a strange dark figure appeared ahead of him. It rode not a horse, but a goat! The creature sat backwards upon the animal so that he could stare

into the knight's face. With sudden horror the knight recognized him. It was the Devil himself, grinning with fierce pleasure, and beckoning to him.

The knight tried to stop his horse, but the animal acted as if it were in a trance, following the goat. The two riders went over the drawbridge of the castle, their mounts' hoofs echoing on the planks like the sound of doom. There was no one about; everyone had fled at the sight of the Devil.

"What do you want of me?" the knight cried.

The Devil laughed, and the knight shivered at the sound. Before his eyes, his great castle began to sink into the earth, and he felt the ground giving way beneath his horse. Down, down, fathoms deep they sank, into the cold dark ground. The earth swallowed them up, and the castle, the knight, and his horse were never seen again.

⇒ Why Bears Eat Meat ⇐

Long ago bears were not the ferocious meat-eaters they are today. In those times there were no better friends on earth than men and bears. They worked together and they divided what they produced. This happy arrangement might have gone on forever if it had not been for a certain sly farmer.

One day the man and his bear friend were planting wheat. The man was highly pleased with their work and he looked about him happily.

"Now, Bruin," he said, "all we have to worry about is how to divide the wheat when it's ripe. That is going to be hard. But I think I have a solution to the problem. Suppose you take the bottom half of the crop and I take the top half. What do you say?"

"That's all right with me," Bruin rumbled. "If we do that, we'll not get into any arguments."

But when autumn came and they harvested the crop, the bear was dismayed. His friend had all of the thick, full ears of wheat, and he had only the stalks to nibble on! The bear grew hungrier and hungrier as the winter passed, and the hungrier he grew the more angry he became.

"That was a mean trick," he told the man. "You had no right to do that. You are living well, but I am so hungry that I'm getting thin."

"Now don't whine," the man said. "You were pleased enough with the bargain when we made it. You agreed to everything I said, and we did divide the crop equally, didn't we?"

"Yes, but—" Bruin began. The man had already walked away.

"Just wait until next year," the bear muttered to himself.

When spring came, the bear was so weak he could hardly walk. Nevertheless, he was ready to do his share of the planting. The man, looking fat and prosperous, said pleasantly, "Well, what are we going to do this year about dividing our crop?"

"I've thought of that," Bruin said eagerly. "Last year you took the top half and I the bottom half of the harvest. This year I want the top half, and you must take the bottom."

The man nodded. "Very well."

"What's more," Bruin said, "we're not going to plant wheat again. This time I want turnips."

"Good, good!" his friend exclaimed. "Let's get to work."

So they planted turnips, row after row of them. When they had finished, Bruin was very tired but he comforted himself by thinking of the harvest to come. He would live like a king all winter.

"They're coming up nicely," he would say every time he walked out to look at the field. "They're almost ready."

Finally the day of the harvest came. The two workers pulled up the juicy turnips. They piled them on the ground and the pile was as high as Bruin himself. Suddenly, as he looked at it, his face fell. If they stuck to their bargain, he would have only a lot of worthless leaves and stems, and the man would have all of the delicious, scrunchy turnips.

The bear pointed a paw at the farmer.

"What's the matter?" the man asked.

"You know what's the matter!" Bruin roared. "You've cheated me again! From now on, I'll have nothing more to do with you."

He lumbered off to the woods. That was the day bears began to eat meat, and they have done it ever since.

⚚ *The Man in the Moon* ⚚

NEAR THE BIG CITY OF GRONINGEN there lived a farmer named
Piet. He was different from his neighbors, who were also
farmers, for he was dishonest and greedy. When he took his
vegetables to the market place in Groningen, he tried to sell
them to newly married young women. They didn't know as
much about marketing as the older women, and he could fool
them more easily. Piet sold his wilted vegetables as fresh ones,
and he charged far too much for his fresh ones.

The other farmers who brought their vegetables to the market place in their carts, prided themselves on their faithful
customers who came back week after week. But Piet was always trying to sell his produce to strangers who knew nothing
about him. After the women had been cheated by him several

times, they did not come back, and if they saw him, they turned their heads and crossed the street.

This didn't bother Piet. He sat by his vegetable cart with a smug expression on his face. "At home," he thought, "I have stockings full of gold and silver. I have just bought another piece of fine land. I have a barn full of cows and new calves. I am richer than any of my neighbors."

One evening, as dusk was falling, he saw a woman coming toward his stall. Piet could tell that she was newly married by the hesitant way she looked at the vegetables; she was not quite sure of their worth. The moon was just rising, but its light was still rather weak, and it was hard for her to see the wilted lettuce lying on the stall.

"Lettuce, mevrouw?" Piet asked the young woman who carried an empty basket on her arm.

"Is it fresh?"

"Of course, mevrouw. And not too dear for this time of year. Only fourteen stuivers a head."

"My husband is so fond of lettuce, but— Now, you're not fooling me, farmer? This lettuce is really fresh?"

He looked indignant. "Fooling you? I? Why do you ask that? If I'm deceiving you, mevrouw, I hope I fly to the moon!"

The words were hardly out of his mouth when, cart and all, Piet rose into the air. While the young woman clasped her hands and screamed, he flew straight to the moon—and there he was held fast.

In case you didn't know how the man in the moon got there, this is the story. And you may be sure that no other farmer ever tried to fool anyone in the market place of Groningen after that, because he was afraid *he* might become a man in the sun!

⤳ The House with the Heads ⤴

In Amsterdam there is a great house with four heads carved of stone on its wall. To those who ask why the heads are there, Amsterdammers tell this story.

Long ago, when every man had to guard his own house and possessions, a rich man and his wife had a cook called Maartje. One night when her master and mistress were out, the cook sat alone in the kitchen. She was a young, fair-haired girl who took her work seriously. Tonight she had been told to guard mevrouw's jewels and mijnheer's money, and she was proud of being trusted with this task. And Maartje was so thrifty that she sat in the dark without even a lighted candle to keep her company.

114

She did not mind being alone—it was rather pleasant to sit in the big comfortable kitchen with nothing to do. Occasionally she heard a passerby's footsteps on the cobbled street, or a boy singing as he rowed down one of the curving canals of Amsterdam.

Suddenly she sat up straight and listened. There was a faint noise somewhere in the house. Her employers had told her to guard their valuables, and she would do it. She lit a candle and watched its wavering light make shadows on the wall as she went from room to room.

Maartje looked in the dark corners, and behind the big chests. She went up into the attic, dim and frightening with only a faint gleam of moonlight coming through the tiny window. She looked in her own small room, which her mistress had made so pleasant for her. She peered behind the heavy curtains in case somebody might be lurking there.

When she stopped to listen, she heard the noise again. There was no one on the upper floors. Perhaps someone was in the cellar. Maartje blew out her candle and quietly crept down the cellar steps, as silently as if *she* were a thief. Holding her own breath to listen, she heard the sound of breathing somewhere in the darkness.

Whoever it is, she thought, he is somewhere in this cellar. She flattened herself against the wall, listening. In the dimness she saw the moonlight coming through a small square opening that led to the street. A hoarse voice said, "You go first!"

The girl knew that the window opening was just big enough for a man's head and shoulders to get through, and if they could get through, his body could follow.

She hurried up the cellar steps to the kitchen and came back almost at once with a long, sharp carving knife clutched in her hand. A head had already appeared in the window. She went close and whispered, "Don't be afraid. I'll take you by the shoulder and help you through. There's plenty to steal, and I know where all the valuables are."

The thief grinned happily. This was an unexpected piece of luck. He struggled until he got his shoulders through the opening. At that same instant Maartje grabbed him by his hair and, with one powerful sweep of her knife, cut off his head.

She pulled his body through the window and tossed it to one side. *That* one was disposed of!

Then she looked up, and said softly, "*He* got through. Now it's your turn. Don't worry, I'll help you, too."

Even as she spoke, the second thief began working himself into the opening. She grasped him by his long hair and laughed. "We'll divide everything, eh? I'm alone in the house. My mistress has beautiful jewels. Which do you like better, diamonds or pearls?"

She pulled him forward and he thought she was trying to help him. "You're going to see more gold and silver than you ever saw in your life. When my master and mistress come home they'll be surprised to find how much I managed to take away—with your help."

As soon as she had him through the opening, she cut off his head, too, and threw it into a corner. Then she got ready for the third thief.

"Your friends are getting what they deserve, and you're going to get it, too," she told him. And, pushing and pulling, she helped him through the window until she could cut off *his* head.

When the fourth head appeared in the window, she said, "Don't worry! You'll get just what the others got. I'll not give one of you any more than I gave the others." And she used her sharp knife on him.

There were no more thieves outside. It was quiet again.

Maartje got her candle from the kitchen and held it high. The cellar was strewn with four heads and four lifeless bodies. She went to the window, and called out, "Is there anybody else there? If there is, speak up! I'll do as much for you as I did for these."

There was no answer. She was tired, but she went slowly up the steps to the kitchen, and sat down to wait for her master and mistress.

At last she heard their carriage drive up. Maartje unlocked the door. Her employers came in and greeted her, then walked into the big parlor. Mevrouw went over to the chest where she kept her jewels, and lifted the lid. Her gold chains and diamond rings blinked up at her. "Tomorrow I must rearrange these," she said. "It is late now; let us go to bed."

She took up the silver table bell and rang it. Maartje came to stand in the doorway.

"Did anything happen while we were away?" asked her mistress.

"Yes, mevrouw. Thieves were here."

"Thieves!" The woman looked as if she couldn't believe her ears.

"In the cellar," Maartje explained. "Would mevrouw and mijnheer like to see for themselves?"

They looked at one another in bewilderment. Had Maartje taken leave of her senses? But they took up candles and followed her. On the cellar floor they saw the four lifeless bodies and the four heads.

When mijnheer found his voice, he cried, "Who did this?"

"I did," Maartje said modestly. They gazed at her with amazement. What a wonderful maidservant they had! How seriously she took her trust!

By the next day the story had spread all over Amsterdam, and for days after that people could talk of nothing else—how one young woman had killed four desperate and stalwart thieves. It was incredible!

Mijnheer and mevrouw wondered for months how they could do honor to Maartje, and at last they decided to have four heads carved of stone, to be placed along the façade of their house, so that everyone could know what had taken place there. And to this day the house is known as "the House with the Heads."

But Maartje never could understand why all the fuss was made about her, or why people thought she had done anything unusual.

☙ The Punishment ☚

In the year 1315 there was a great famine in the land. And in Leyden it was worst of all. Hunger was killing family after family there. The townspeople starved in the streets. The mothers had no milk for their children.

There were two sisters in the city of Leyden, Anne and Marie, who had always lived together, happily enough, until Marie fell in love and married. Anne lived alone then, and it seemed as if nothing had changed between them, but behind her smile there was envy and jealousy.

Hunger came first to the homes of the poor. Marie gave to them with full hands, and the poor blessed her with their words of thanks.

Day after day the famine grew worse. Now not only the

poor, but the highly placed, the well-to-do, and the masters of the guilds felt the pinch of hunger. Marie and her husband went out every day with baskets of food on their arms. To whomever asked, they gave.

One evening Marie heard a timid knocking on her door— *klop, klop, klop*—three times.

"Don't open it!" her husband said fearfully. "It may be robbers."

"Whoever knocks so softly," Marie answered, "has more need than one who knocks loudly." She opened the door. There stood her sister.

"Marie," Anne cried, "in the name of God, help me! I haven't eaten in three days."

"Is all your bread gone?" Marie asked, amazed.

"Yes. Everything I had I gave to the poor. There is nothing left."

"Come in, come in, and sit with us. You are one of us. If we have enough for six, we can make it enough for seven."

Marie gave her bread and meat. It was very little, but it was enough.

"Eat and drink, Anne," her sister said warmly, "and stay with us. You must not go away again; we will take care of you."

"No, no," Anne said, "I want to be in my own house. What would people say if I came to stay with you? You have given to the poor, and everyone knows it. I have given to them, too, but secretly. People don't know of my good deeds, and so no one will believe that I am poor. Let me come here after dark. I will knock softly three times, as I did tonight. Then you will know that it's poor Anne. 'She's hungry,' you will say, 'and she's standing there outside.' "

Marie said warmly, "As long as we have anything to eat, my dear, you shall share it with us—to the very last crumb."

The next evening, as she waited for Anne, Marie stood near the door. She wanted to spare her sister the shame of having to stand at the door till it was opened. And afterward she saw to it that Anne went with her through the streets of the city, giving out bread as if they were doing it together. People praised the two sisters, one as much as the other.

The famine grew worse. People had to pay with gold for a handful of flour. Then came the time when everyone was looking out for himself, without a care for what was happening to his neighbor. Dead fish floated on the water, the cattle died of a strange sickness, the grass was burned and dry. The bleak earth was covered by a gray sky. Day followed day, and there was no end to the terrible famine.

Marie gave generously from her dwindling store of food. One evening, when she was portioning out the bread to her husband and children and Anne, she herself took nothing.

When they had finished, Anne said, "Can't you give me a few more pieces of bread? I am still very hungry."

"I can't," her sister said. "There is no more bread."

"Then bake some."

"I have no flour."

"Can't you buy it?"

"If I had money, yes. But I have no money. We, too, are as poor as the rest now."

Anne stood up angrily. "You selfish woman!" she cried. "Why did you give another piece of bread to that beggar today? Why did you give away your money? Oh, I know you and your wiles! Putting on airs so that people will say, 'the good Marie,' while they think, 'that wicked Anne!' That's why you were so generous all the time—so that you could belittle me! That was always your aim, for as long as I can remember —ever since you married, and left me alone."

Marie bent her head as though she were guilty of these

charges. At last she said softly, "Oh, Anne, how wrong you are! How you twist things!"

"I'm not twisting anything! I will never set foot in your house again. Now I see you for what you really are."

Without another word she left the house.

At last there came a day when there was no food in Marie's house and she was obliged to beg. She appealed to some of the people whom she had helped before.

One of them said to her, "Go to your sister. She has flour enough! She won't give any to us, but to you she will, of course!"

"My sister has no bread. She gave it all away. She told me so."

"Your sister has no bread! That makes me laugh. Don't believe her! Go and see for yourself!"

Marie said, "Even if you speak the truth, I cannot go near her. My sister hates me, and she would give me nothing. She thinks I did her a wrong."

"Well, I have nothing for you, either." And the door was shut in her face.

When the people she had helped refused her, Marie begged from strangers. They refused her, too, for they had nothing to spare. Every day she came home with empty hands.

Her husband died, and three of her children, and she was left with only one son.

He was little, and he cried all the time! "Mother! Give me bread!"

"There is no bread, my dear one."

"Go and get some, Mother!"

Marie held the child close. "Don't die, darling! My only one!"

"Mother, give me bread. Bread, bread, bread!"

That evening she went to her sister's house. She knocked softly three times on the door— *klop, klop, klop.*

No one answered. She listened to hear if someone was coming. There was no sound. Again she knocked on the door, as a beggar might knock, timidly, softly—*klop, klop, klop.*

Still there was no answer. "My poor sister," Marie thought. "She, too, has had to go out begging. People lied when they said she had flour to bake bread."

She hurried home. Her child lay on the floor, too weak to move. "Mother," he whispered, "did you bring me something to eat? I'm so hungry, Mother! Bread!"

"I have none to give you, my only one." She sank down and tried to comfort him.

It was then that she seemed to hear a voice speaking to her from afar. "Go tomorrow in the early evening to your sister Anne. She has the bread you need. Your good works are known in heaven, and you shall be blessed."

Marie hesitated before saying, "Anne sat at my table and ate my food. Surely she would not have done that if she could bake her own bread?"

The voice answered her softly, "Have faith."

Marie wept for joy. She hugged her child and promised him, "Tomorrow we shall have bread. Tomorrow!"

The next day, as soon as dusk fell, she made herself ready and went to her sister's house. It took her longer than usual to reach it, for she was cold and weak with hunger. But the thought of her child waiting at home drove her on. At her sister's house the door was partly open, and the wonderful fragrance of baking bread was wafted to the street.

"Anne!" Marie cried happily. "Anne, did someone give you a present of flour? I suppose you were planning to come and share it with me, as I did mine with you. You'll forgive whatever you think I did wrong, won't you, Anne? We are so hungry!"

Anne looked at her distantly. "What do you want of me? I did not tell you to come here."

"But, sister, my child is starving!"

"Your child? You dare speak to me of *one* child?"

Marie cried, "Surely you know that my husband and my three other children died of starvation? Now I have only this one left. I beg you, on my knees, to save him."

Anne stared at her in silence.

"I'm not asking anything for myself, just for my child. Believe me! If you have only a little, divide what you have between yourself and the boy."

"I have no bread."

"Anne, how can you say that? The smell of fresh bread is in the air. It smells so good!"

"I swear to you I have no bread."

Marie sank to her knees. She clung to Anne's dress. "Sister, you are lying to me. How can you do this? Don't you know that you will never be forgiven? For the sake of your soul, give me bread!"

Anne loosened Marie's hands and stepped back. Her voice was cold. "If it is true that I have bread, let it be turned to stone. If it is true that I have flour, let it be turned to stone in my fingers as I bake."

Marie stood up. She put her hands over her heart and said slowly, "If it is true that you have bread, let it be turned to stone. If it is true that you have flour, let it be turned to stone in your fingers as you bake. Amen."

She left the house and went down the street, without looking back.

As soon as she had disappeared, Anne closed and bolted the

door. She walked quickly towards the kitchen where she had been baking. She smiled to herself.

"It's all for me. Just for me. No one else shall touch it."

She took up one of the brown loaves that lay cooling on the table. Her fingers felt cold.

Her voice rose in a shriek. "Stone!"

All her loaves had turned to stone. Anne looked wildly around the room. She would bake others; she would bake twice as many. She went to the closet where the flour was hidden. When she ran the flour through her fingers, it turned to stone.

She thought frantically "But I still have gold! I have plenty of money. I will buy more flour." She opened the chest where she hid her money and took out a bag of it. She went to the miller and he demanded the whole bag of money for a small bag of flour, but she paid him willingly. Now she could bake fresh bread.

When she entered her house again, the bag felt unusually heavy. Fearfully she opened it. The flour had turned to stone.

The house was full of gold, but it did her no good. No one had food to spare, and her own words were bitter in her mouth, for she knew what lay ahead of her.

But when Marie returned to her own house, she found flour in abundance, and loaves of fresh bread on the table. She cut slices of it and watched her son eat them. Then she gave to the poor, and at last she sat down to eat some herself.

❧ The Simple Maid of Hunsingoo ❧

THE COAT-OF-ARMS of the town of Hunsingoo shows a knight and a maiden on a brown horse, followed by a star. Winsum has the same crest on its town hall. And when people ask what it means, this is the story they hear:

Long ago, a young girl called Kerstine lived with her family in the neighborhood of Hunsingoo. Kerstine was a contented maiden with no desire for riches or fame. She looked forward only to falling in love someday, being married, and having children of her own. Kerstine was so modest that she did not realize how beautiful she was. Her hair was as golden as ripe grain, her eyes as blue as cornflowers, and she had graceful white hands.

Near Hunsingoo was the castle of a rich young knight, Rolf,

whose ancestry was so noble that his coat-of-arms had many quarterings upon it, showing that he was related to a great number of important families. But the knight himself was a scoundrel. He thought of nothing but pleasure and having his own way. Peer, his squire, was as much of a scoundrel as Rolf.

One dark day when Rolf was wondering what new mischief he could do, Peer said to him, "You've never seen that beautiful maiden, Kerstine, who lives near Hunsingoo, have you?"

Rolf was surprised. "I thought I knew every beautiful maiden in this neighborhood. Why have I not seen Kerstine?"

"Yesterday she was only a child," Peer said, "but today she is a lovely young woman."

"Like the madeliefjes that flower suddenly in May?"

"Yes. Would you like to meet her?" Peer asked.

"Of course," Rolf answered. And the following day they rode over to her father's house and dismounted. Kerstine came to the door.

"I am thirsty," said the knight. "Give me a draught of water."

Kerstine's parents knew of Rolf's reputation. Still, they could not refuse him a drink of water.

Kerstine went to the well to fill the pail. Rolf followed her, and watched her as she let out the chain. He leaned on the stone coping.

"I can see your beautiful reflection deep in the well," he said.

She laughed. "How can you? Deep in the well there is nothing but darkness."

"I can see it because my eyes are filled with it, and I can see nothing else."

"You must not talk that way," she protested, but without

anger. "I am only a simple maiden, and it is wrong to speak as if I were anything else."

He said, "Do you know what I am going to call you? Madelief! You are like a lovely daisy just come into bloom."

She drew back. "Here is your beaker of water," she said.

While he drank, she disappeared into the house.

Rolf was not discouraged. Every day he followed Kerstine. If she went to the meadow to milk the cows, he was there. If she walked through the woods to gather faggots, he appeared upon his brown horse. If she went to the brook to pick watercress, he leaned against a tree to watch her.

And always he told her how beautiful she was, and how much he loved her. But she would not listen to him, because she knew that he was fickle. No one had a good word to say for him.

One day, when he met her on the road, he stood directly in front of her, and tried to catch her. But she was too quick for him and that made him angry. "How dare you run from me?"

She tossed her head. "Has the hawk no other prey?" And with that, she ran past him.

His friends began to make sport of him, for the tale of his rejection was spreading far and wide. "Can't you catch the little dove?" they taunted him.

"Just wait," Rolf answered furiously. "If she won't come willingly, she'll come *unwillingly!*"

Kerstine heard of this, but she was not frightened. He need not think he could scare her with his threats.

But Rolf began plotting, day and night, for some way to win her for his own. One evening, when he was sitting alone in the great hall of his castle, Peer came to him.

"Master," he said excitedly, "now is the time!"

"The time for what?"

"Her father and mother, her brother and sisters, have all gone to a feast, and Kerstine is alone in the house."

Rolf jumped up. "Saddle my brown horse, and come along! We'll catch her this time!"

Peer gave his master a hand up, and they rode swiftly to Kerstine's house. Peer found a ladder and set it against the wall. He climbed up to her window and tapped on it.

"What is it?" Kerstine called from inside.

Peer made his voice sound like her brother's. "I came back early. Let me in! The others are still at the feast."

She opened the window, and Peer leapt inside and caught her in his arms. Then he dragged her, struggling, down the ladder, and placed her in front of Rolf on the brown horse. The knight put spurs to his steed, and off he galloped.

"Where are you taking me, lord knight?" Kerstine asked. Her voice held no fear.

"To my castle," he answered. "You shall have the most beautiful room for your own."

"I don't want the most beautiful room in your castle," Kerstine said. "I like my little room at home."

"I will cover your beautiful throat with pearls, my little Madelief," Rolf promised.

"I don't care for pearls," she said.

"Servants will surround you. You will only have to clap your hands, and whatever you wish shall be done."

"I don't want servants," Kerstine said. "I like to work."

"You will rest on cushions of silk and velvet. You will wear gold and diamond bracelets on your arms. And your little feet will be shod with satin slippers."

"I don't want cushions of silk and velvet," Kerstine said. "I don't care at all for gold and diamond bracelets. And I couldn't walk in slippers."

The brown horse galloped into the woods. "See how beautiful the moonlight is on the moss," the knight said. "Soon we shall be at the castle."

"Let me go!" she ordered.

"I would rue it forever if I let you go."

Kerstine said vigorously, "And you'll rue it forever if you *don't* let me go!"

Rolf threw back his head and laughed. The sound of his laughter floated through the forest. And while he laughed, Kerstine stretched out her sturdy foot, and with all her young strength lifted him right out of the saddle. He fell to the ground and lay there motionless.

Kerstine took the reins in her hands, turned the brown horse around, and rode swiftly back to her home. It was near morning when she reached the house.

Her father cried, "Where have you been?"

When she told him, he would not believe her. No one would believe her. How could she, a young girl, unseat a powerful knight from his horse? It was impossible!

"Go and see for yourselves," she said proudly. "You'll find him easily enough. He is lying under the trees near the edge of the forest. He had a heavy fall, and I doubt if he has come to yet."

The news spread. Every man who knew Rolf, or knew of him, took to his horse and went to the place where the forest began. Sure enough, there lay the knight on the moss. All of his enemies laughed, and his friends, too. Peer came running, and lifted his master to his feet and led him to his castle.

Now at that time the people of Hunsingoo wanted a coat-of-arms, but they lacked a subject for one. When they heard this story, they had one. An artist drew a horse with a knight and maiden riding on it. He drew a star, to show that it was night, and placed it behind the riders to indicate that the maiden had not gone with the knight willingly. Her hair hung loose as a sign that she had been carried away against her will.

When Rolf saw this coat-of-arms, he decided never to go near Hunsingoo again. And Peer, his squire, avoided that neighborhood, too, where the young maidens were so "simple."

≥ The Rich Widow of Stavoren ≤

STAVOREN, on the Zuider Zee, was once one of the proudest cities in the land. It was so rich and important that even the doors of the houses were of solid gold. The ships that crowded its harbor had sailed the seven seas. The people of other cities envied Stavoren for its beauty and wealth, and those who lived there felt that nothing could ever lessen their prosperity.

In the city lived a very rich widow. She was beautiful and vain, and always looking for ways to impress people with her wealth.

One day, when her largest ship was starting on a long voyage, she called the captain to her.

"Captain," she said, "while you are away, I want you to hunt for the most precious thing in the world. Something more

133

precious than has ever been created by human hands. No matter how costly it is, I want you to buy it and bring it to me. Then everyone will envy me and do me honor."

"But, noble lady," the captain said in a worried voice, "how shall I know what is the most precious thing in the world? Isn't there someone else to whom you can give this task?"

"No, you are the oldest captain in my service. You have made more voyages and longer voyages than any of the others. You are the one to do it. As for knowing the right thing to buy, when you see something and you say to yourself, 'Behold, this is the most precious thing in the world,' then you will know that is what I want. Buy it and bring it to me. But if you do not find it, Captain, you need never return to this port. Now go!"

"I will do my best," the old man said, with a weary shake of his head. "But I don't know where I shall ever find it."

Far and wide, the captain sailed, visiting many strange and distant places, and always looking for the treasure the noble lady had told him to buy. The ship's hold was filled with gold she had given him. But though he had the money to pay for it, he could not find anything rare enough to buy for the widow.

He saw diamonds, and brocades, satins and laces, Oriental rugs as soft as silk, chased gold work, and beautiful bracelets and rings—but all had been fashioned by human hands and other human hands could make them again. If he returned with any of these things, people would mock the noble lady who had sent him out to bring back the most precious treasure in the world.

He told every trader and storekeeper, "Show me the most precious thing you have." But when they showed him their wares, he would shake his head and say, "No, that's not what I'm looking for."

At last he came to a big city he had never visited before. He went to the goldsmiths there, but he found nothing to buy. Finally he decided to leave the city and go farther north, for he had heard of a place where furs, more beautiful and costly than ermine, were sold; he would buy them and take them back to Stavoren.

But on his last morning in the city, as he was passing an old, ramshackle building, the captain stopped short. In the building he saw the treasure he was looking for—better than gold or silver, more precious than anything made by man!

"Now at last I've found it!" he cried happily. "Whatever price they ask, I will pay. For this has more worth than all the gold in the hold of my ship—yea, more than all the gold in the world!"

He went inside and bought the contents of the warehouse and had it carried to his ship and stored in the hold. An hour later he sailed for home.

The rich widow of Stavoren could hardly wait for his return. What would he bring her? She looked at her white hands; she touched her golden hair. A smile played around her lips as she thought how her loveliness would be made even lovelier by the treasure that the captain was bringing her.

And she couldn't help boasting to her women friends, "Other ships from Stavoren are laden with cargoes of wood or fish, but *my* ship is laden with nothing but gold. I know you are all rich, but none of you has ever seen as much gold as I sent out with my captain. And whatever he buys with it shall be all mine."

One morning there was shouting in the streets. Her ship had returned! Everyone in Stavoran ran to the harbor, laughing and talking, and trying to guess what the cargo might be.

The widow hurried to the wharf and called out, "Tell me, what did you bring me, Captain?"

"Noble lady," he answered happily, "I have brought you wheat! Such beautiful wheat you have never seen before!"

He waited for her to thank him. Hadn't he brought her the most precious thing in the world, something that no human hands could make? But the widow was furious. Instead of being able to dazzle the townspeople with her treasure, she would become the laughingstock of Stavoren! She must do something—quickly—so that they could not laugh at her.

"Wheat!" she said. "You dared to bring me wheat? Where is it?"

"In the ship's hold, noble lady," he replied.

She raised her arm haughtily. "Then," she commanded, "have it brought up and thrown into the sea!"

The captain was horrified. "Noble lady," he protested, "only sorrow will come to us if you order that to be done."

She stripped a ruby ring from her finger and tossed it into the water. "Sooner will my ring return to me than sorrow will come to Stavoren!" she said. "Do as I say!"

He could hardly believe his ears, but he dared not disobey her. Sadly he had the wheat thrown overboard into the Zuider Zee.

The rich widow went back to her house, thinking of the treasure she had lost because of her foolish captain. But she had other ships, and when they returned she would fill *their* holds with gold, and send *their* captains on the same quest.

The next morning, while she was combing her golden hair before the mirror, her cook burst into the room. "Mevrouw!" the woman cried, her face white. "Look what I found! It was in the fish I bought at market for your dinner. When I cut it open, there was—this!" She held up the ruby ring, which the widow had thrown into the sea the day before.

The widow snatched it from her. "I will hide it, and no one will know. See that you keep silence, too."

But, though she hid it, the ring had returned, and with it came ill fortune. Word came that her other ships had been lost in a terrible storm. And not only the widow but all of Stavoren suffered. For every grain of wheat that had been tossed into the sea, a grain of sand appeared. The sand drifted in and piled up in the harbor—higher and higher. The harbor that had once been open to the big ships of the world was closed by the sand to all but the smallest boats. Poverty and hunger came to Stavoren, and the people thought longingly of the wheat that had been thrown into the sea. And the poorest and hungriest of all was the widow.

The next summer grain began to grow in the sand. The townspeople were overjoyed, because they thought that a new prosperity would be theirs. They would harvest the grain and divide it, and then there would be no more hunger and poverty in Stavoren.

But, when they went to harvest it, they found that it was nothing but straw. There was not a grain of wheat in the full heads. Not a single grain. And though they cut down the wheat, the sand remained, and Stavoren never again became the proud, rich city it had been. Instead it dreams through the sunlight of summer and through the raw, dark days of winter, one of the Dead Cities of the Zuider Zee.

⇗ The Shell Grotto of Nienoort ⇖

ONCE UPON A TIME, the castle of Nienoort had an incredible treasure-room. Vast amounts of gold and silver were stored in it, and there were chests full of diamonds and pearls and golden goblets filled with topazes and opals, rubies and emeralds. Bracelets lay there in glittering beauty, and there were forty-five marvelously wrought necklaces.

Not many people had seen this rich treasure-room—only a few men, and almost no women.

Near Nienoort there lived a woman who had once had a fleeting glimpse of the room as the door was being closed, and ever since then she could think of nothing else. "The treasure-room," she would sigh to herself. "I must see it again!"

She managed to meet and make friends with Grietje, the

small daughter of the castle watchman. People often saw them together, hand in hand, wandering over the fields, talking and laughing. The young woman always brought the child some treat—a piece of fruit, or some delicious sweet. She knew all kinds of stories and games. She could sing lovely songs, and she could recognize any bird by its color and the way it flew. Grietje's father trusted her.

"They're both just children," he thought indulgently, when he saw them together.

One fine summer evening he went down to the lake to go rowing. But first he told his daughter that no one should go into the treasure-room, and that she must warn the lord of the castle if she saw any stranger in the neighborhood.

He had no sooner gone than the woman called Grietje to her. But on this particular evening the woman did not play with the child. She stroked her head, as she said softly, "Is your father away?"

"Yes."

"Where did he go?"

"Oh, he's rowing on the lake."

The woman caught her breath, and asked, "Then are you all alone? How soon is your father coming back?"

"He'll be very late, I think. I have to stay nearby, because I must guard the treasure-room."

"Is the treasure-room beautiful? Are there lovely things in it?"

Grietje clasped her hands. "You never saw such beautiful things! It's light in there . . . lighter than when the sun shines, and all the stones have light in them."

The woman said gently, "Won't you open the door for a moment, so that I can see all that light?"

The woman was her good friend, Grietje thought. She went to get the key. It was a long, heavy key, and it took all of the little girl's strength to put it into the lock and turn it seven times to the left, and then half a turn to the right. The door opened without a sound, and they both went into the room. The child laid the heavy key on a small table near the door.

At first the woman thought how easy it would be to steal some of the jewels and take them far away. The man she wanted to marry was poor. There were so many jewels here, a few of them would never be missed. She stood staring at the bins and beakers full of precious stones.

"Come!" Grietje begged. "Let's go outside and play!"

The woman gave her no answer.

"Come to us," the glittering jewels seemed to say. "Take us in your hands." She longed for them, but it was as if she were rooted to the floor. She could not move.

"Come play with me," the child begged again.

But the jewels were speaking to the woman: "Soon it will be night. You won't be able to see us then. Come closer. Touch us. Take us in your hands. See how beautiful and rare we are. Come!"

Grietje caught her by the hand and tried to pull her towards the door. "Let's go out and play together. Please!"

The woman stroked the child's hair and kissed her. "Go along, dear. I will come soon."

Grietje was eager to get outside. She ran toward the door, and when she saw the key on the little table, she thought what fun it would be to play a joke on her friend. She put the heavy key in the lock and turned it. The big bolts slid into place. The door was locked fast. She stooped and called through the keyhole, "See that you come soon! I'm going to play by myself."

A little butterfly flew past her shoulder. She turned and ran after it. When it lighted on a flower she tried to catch it, but the butterfly fluttered away across the fields and into the woods. Farther and farther Grietje went, always trying to catch the butterfly that was as beautiful as any jewel.

After a while Grietje grew tired and as it was getting dark, she made her way home again and fell into bed, after saying her prayers, and fell fast asleep. She was so tired that when her father came home she did not wake up.

Meanwhile, the woman stood in the dark treasure-room. With the closing of the door all the light had departed, and the precious stones did not speak to her any more. The diamonds had become part of the night, the gold did not glisten. She was in the midst of untold treasures, but she could not see them. Wearily she fell to the ground and slept.

With the first rays of morning light in the treasure-room the stones began to shimmer and sparkle again. "Now it is day," they said to her. "Come to us. Take us in your hands. Put us on your fingers and around your throat."

The woman could not resist these words. Wandering from table to chest she took up the gems. She smiled as she wound priceless strands of pearls around her neck and put five diamond bracelets on her arm, to glitter with her every movement. At last she decided to go. Only when she got to the door did she find that Grietje had locked her in.

The guards discovered her there. Grietje had wakened and told her father that she had only meant to tease her friend by locking her in the room. The guards rushed to the treasure-room and there she was—her throat wound with pearls, the bracelets glistening on her arms. The men seized her roughly by the shoulders and hurried her before the lord of the castle.

The lord of the castle looked at her sternly. She tried to tell him how, for months, she had longed to get inside the treasure-room and how at last luck had been with her. But when she told him that she had only wanted to *see* the jewels, it sounded like a lie. She was sure that she would be condemned to death.

Her head was bowed in fear, and she could almost feel the sharp edge of the sword. She shuddered and whispered, "I'm too young to die! My life is still ahead of me! I don't want to die!"

The lord of the castle looked at her long and hard. "Why did you try to steal?" he asked her.

She said in a low voice, "I wanted to go far away, to another land, with my belovéd. But when I saw the pearls and diamonds, I couldn't move. I might have been miles from here, and no one would ever have found me—"

Her answer made the lord of the castle very angry.

"I know a better punishment for you than death. I shall have all the jewels taken out of the treasure-room, and you will make it into a grotto of shells. You will begin with the first rays of the sun and until it is finished you will see no human being. That is to be your punishment."

The following day the woman began her task. In the night the guards had removed the precious stones and gold, and in their place left thousand of shells, of all colors and shapes.

In the distance the woman could hear voices, but no one came near her. Sometimes she thought she heard the voice of the man she had loved and hoped to marry. It was for him that she had planned to steal some of the jewels. When she thought she heard his voice, her hands trembled and her eyes filled with tears. But then she would return to her work, so that she would soon be done. Surely this would not last long, and she could enjoy the rest of her years with her belovéd.

Day after day went by. Sometimes she thought that the shells she held in her hand were diamonds and pearls, topazes and rubies, and she lifted them up to catch the light. She made a work of art with the shells on the walls of the treasure-room.

She thought to herself, "When the door opens in the morning, I will hurry away and take some of these precious jewels with me. Then he and I—my belovéd and I—will go to a strange land, and there we will marry. I'll just take one necklace—"

But the next morning she went on with her endless task. She put shell after shell into place until she had used almost all of them. When there were only a few left, a trap door in the ceiling opened and masses of shells were thrown into the room; but this she did not know. It seemed to the woman that the shells were the jewels she had first seen here—and loved. Even so, there came a day when the pile of shells dwindled—and then was gone.

"Now I will be free!" she thought, and her heart beat fiercely.

The door opened. She walked out and saw the sunlight. Children were playing on the grass. A little goat was tied nearby. Everything looked just as it had when she entered the treasure-room. And yet she didn't recognize any of these children.

She was free! Now she would go to find her belovéd. But how strange it was that she couldn't find the way to her home. All of the houses and even the roads looked different. What had happened during the year she had worked in the treasure-room?

A young girl met her on the path. How familiar she looked! Wasn't this the little girl with whom she had played? The woman began to laugh. How the child had grown in this short time! Would Grietje still know her, now that she had put up her hair? She called, "Grietje!"

The young woman stood still. "That's not my name," she said gently, "but I knew her very well—the woman you're calling."

"Knew her? Who are you, then?"

"I am her granddaughter."

The woman cried, "Her granddaughter!" And suddenly she had a dreadful thought.

She ran to the lake and leaned over the water and looked at herself as in a mirror.

She saw gray hair, a wrinkled face and a lined forehead, and deep-sunken eyes. She clasped her hands in anguish. Her whole life had gone by. She was an old, old woman. She had nothing to live for now. Slowly she returned to the treasure-room, and looked once more at the work over which she had labored sixty years—sixty years that had seemed to her no more than one.

On the threshold of the grotto that had once been the treasure-room she sank down, and there they found her the next day. The story says that she is buried somewhere in the shell grotto of Nienoort which she made with her own hands.

⊰ The Curse ⊱

THE COUNT OF CUYNER was a deceitful man. In times of war, when the Count of Holland and the Lord of Friesland were fighting each other, he joined the one who, he thought, had the better chance of winning.

People had a saying: "As untrustworthy as the Count of Cuyner."

The old count was determined that the Cuyners should become as powerful as kings and emperors. His two sons, Jan and Edmond, were very much like their father; they, too, wanted their name to be known as a mighty one, even if they must resort to treachery to make it so.

Now the Count of Holland and the Lord of Friesland were disputing over a piece of land, and both of them had gathered

146

their armies. The Count of Cuyner sent a messenger to the Lord of Friesland, telling him: "Do not be anxious. Where the Lord of Friesland fights, there fights the Count of Cuyner beside him."

So the Lord of Friesland did not fear to meet his enemy. He had forgotten other times when the Count of Cuyner had not lived up to his word. He went forth with his knights and vassals and all of his servants. His banners flew in the breeze and his knights' armor shone in the sun.

The Lord of Friesland knew just what he must do, for the Count of Cuyner had written: "Come to the land of Kuinre. It is full of swamps and morasses. I will help you, and my sons will help you. Wait in the land of Kuinre till the Count of Holland comes towards Friesland with his men."

The wily Count of Cuyner had also sent a messenger to the Count of Holland. "I have lured the Lord of Friesland to the swamps of Kuinre, where I alone know the way. Do not hesitate. . . . I will help you."

When the two armies were drawn up on opposite sides of the treacherous swamps, two riders came to the camp of the Count of Holland and greeted him heartily. They were Edmond and Jan of Cuyner. At dawn the next day, they said, they would lead the Hollanders along dry paths so that they could get through the swamps to surprise and overcome the Frisians.

No one had seen Edmond and Jan leave their father's castle, or met them along the way.

"No one knows of my scheme," the old count thought. He left his castle and went to the encampment of the Lord of Friesland. There he shook the Frisian ruler by the hand and when he was offered a glass of wine he lifted it high and said, "As long as I live, no enemy can come near you. Let us enjoy ourselves tonight. You have nothing to fear!"

The guards stood outside the tent. The night was still and starless. The Count of Cuyner and the Lord of Friesland talked until just before dawn.

Then the count said, "I must leave you now, dear friend. I have promised my two sons to go hunting with them."

He looked across the table. The Lord of Friesland was fast asleep. The wicked old count smiled and slipped quietly out of the tent. He sprang on his waiting horse and rode swiftly into the darkness. His horse did not stumble; it knew its way and started for the castle while the rider gloated over his deception of the Lord of Friesland.

"After a while, he will waken," he said, "but it will be too late. Who will cut off his head for me—Jan or Edmond? Who will bring it to me? I will hold that heavy head in my hands and rejoice, for my land will soon include all of Friesland!"

Suddenly his horse reared. An unearthly voice came out of the early morning light. It sounded like a woman's voice.

"Curséd be your family, Count of Cuyner. Curséd by your name. It will end in one hour, in one day. Now ride to your castle!"

The old man heard the voice, but he laughed as he dug his heel into his horse's side to urge it on. He was not afraid of the sound of a woman's voice mouthing foolish imprecations.

The sun was well up when the Count of Cuyner came to his castle. He went at once to sit on his throne-like chair and wait for news of the battle.

It seemed like a long time before he could cry, "Listen! A messenger is coming!"

But his servants said, "There is no one at the gates."

"The battle should have ended," the count said. "The Frisians must be fighting hard. But they will be overcome."

Late in the afternoon, as shadows were beginning to darken

the corners of the hall, a messenger finally rode up to the castle. He entered silently, and approached the count with slow steps. He took a deep breath before he could begin to speak.

"Before one hour's fighting had taken place, four hundred Hollanders had fallen, and only sixty Frisians," he told the old man.

"That is unbelievable!" said the count.

"Your sons fought with spirit. They were sure of the outcome of the battle."

"Naturally."

"The Lord of Friesland awoke; he hurried from his tent and, even though he was not wearing his armor, he managed to kill seven knights of Holland."

"You lie!" the count cried.

"Your sons, Edmond and Jan, threw themselves upon him. He barely escaped being killed. His men surrounded him to protect him. The Hollanders stormed on, even though their number was far less than that of the Frisians."

"True enough." The Count of Cuyner nodded smugly.

"The Frisians fought well. They overcame the Hollanders finally, and drove them back towards the morasses."

"That—is—not true!" The count's voice rose to a shout.

"Your sons, Edmond and Jan, were caught in the flight, but they called out to each other that they should make a stand—"

"And so they did," the count said eagerly. "Of course they made a stand!"

The messenger's voice went on relentlessly. "And Edmond was killed on the edge of the swamp."

The count cried, "That's the end of your news, surely? Surely Jan was saved. He *was* saved, wasn't he? Tell me he was saved. Perhaps he was badly wounded. But he lives!"

The messenger lowered his eyes so he would not see the count's furious, anxious face. "When Jan saw his brother fall, he stood his ground. He protected himself with his shield, and with his good sword Floreval he laid about him and killed many of his enemies!"

"Ah!" the count said with satisfaction.

The messenger's voice went on. "But what can one man do alone? The Hollanders swept him with them into the swamp. He struggled, but his heavy armor made him sink even deeper than the others—and he drowned."

When he heard this, the Count of Cuyner fell from his chair. Before he died, he remembered the unearthly voice at dawn. In one hour, he had lost his sons, his chance for fame and power. And that same day the Lord of Friesland besieged his castle and became master of his land.

❧ The Two Wishes ❧

EACH CHRISTMAS EVE Saint Peter comes to earth, to take a walk among the villages and find out how people are faring.

It so happened that on this particular cold, snowy night before Christmas he came to a prosperous-looking house and knocked on the front door. A middle-aged woman opened it a crack.

"Good woman—" began Saint Peter.

"Beggars! I am tired of answering the door to beggars!" she said angrily. "You smelled the stew I'm making, no doubt. But it's not for you. If you want to eat stew, you must work for it. Be on your way!" And she slammed the door in his face.

Saint Peter trudged on through the snow. At the far end of the village he saw a thatched cottage with a single light burning in it. He went to the kitchen door this time and knocked softly.

A bent little woman answered, peering into the darkness and holding her lamp high.

"Good woman—" Saint Peter began.

Before he could go on, she cried, "Oh, you poor soul! Your shoes are wet and there's snow on your shoulders. You must be cold to the bone. Come in! I've a bit of a peat fire, and a pot of broth—not much to offer you on a night like this, but you're welcome to what I have."

Saint Peter went into the small room where a meagre fire burned on the hearth. But it was warm and pleasant, and the little old woman bustled about her kitchen, pouring the broth into an earthen bowl, cutting a slice from a homemade loaf, and bringing a pair of old slippers for Saint Peter to put on while she dried his shoes beside the fire.

After a while he got up to go, but she said warmly, "Oh, no, you can't go out in this weather! Wait till morning—perhaps the snow will have stopped by then, and the sun will warm you. My son is away; you can have his bed. Come, I'll light the way."

Saint Peter could not persuade her to let him go on. She saw to it that he was comfortable, and then went to put more peats on the fire.

In the morning she give him breakfast, and before he left her he said, "You have been very good to me, and made me welcome. I cannot repay you, but I can grant you a wish."

"Oh, sir!" she cried.

But he held up his hand. "Do not make your wish now. Think about it a while, and when you have a good wish, say it aloud and it shall be granted."

With that he was gone, and the poor woman spent half the morning trying to think what she should wish for. Then her eyes fell on the big, old-fashioned loom in the corner of the room. Her husband, who was dead, had been a weaver, and there was still a piece of unfinished cloth on the loom, just as he had left it.

"I ought to measure that cloth," she thought. "I wish I knew how much there is." Then she stood still. There was her wish. She said aloud, "May the work I begin tomorrow morning continue all day."

Next morning she began to measure the cloth. When she had twelve yards, she cut it off and rolled it up neatly. Then she saw that the pattern had changed, and the colors were different. She measured that, and there was another twelve yards. She cut it off and rolled it up neatly and set it beside the first roll. She measured and measured—every twelve yards there was a different texture, a different pattern, a different color. The rolls grew and grew. She stacked them along the wall and then in piles on the floor.

The neighbors who came to see what she was doing, could hardly get the door open. All day she measured and measured, and the cloth continued to roll from the loom. By nightfall the cottage was so full that she could scarcely get from the loom to the stove. There was enough cloth to last a lifetime. There was enough to sell in all the neighboring villages and towns. She would never want for money the rest of her life.

"The blessèd stranger!" she said softly, looking around the crowded little room. And she wiped the tears from her eyes with the corner of her apron.

The neighbors spread the news of the miracle that had happened in the poor widow's cottage. The news flew all over town, and of course the woman who had turned Saint Peter away heard it. She was so angry with herself that she shrieked with rage. "How was I to know he could grant a wish?" she cried to her husband. "Why didn't you tell me? Why didn't

he say who he was? He was no ordinary beggar, that's sure.
Oh, misery, misery! I'll not sleep a wink!"

And she didn't. She lay awake all night trying to think how
she could make up for her mistake. If the stranger came again—
But though she kept a sharp watch, he did not appear.

"Maybe he will come again next year," she thought eagerly.
"But it's going to be hard to wait."

All year she busied herself thinking of various things she
would wish for it she were given the chance. And at last she
thought of one that would solve everything. Now all she had
to do was wait till the stranger came back. Oh, how royally
she would treat him!

It was Christmas Eve again when he returned. The moment
she heard a knock that snowy evening the woman was sure it
was the stranger. She flung open the door before he could do
more then knock once.

"Come in, come in!" she cried. Her house was swept and
garnished and polished. A delicious meal was cooking on the
stove. "It's a bad night to be out. You must rest before the
fire, and have supper with us. . . . This is my husband. See,
he will take your cloak and dry it. Dirk, get some more fuel for
the fire, and set another place at the table, and see that the
big bed in the guest room is warmed."

Saint Peter said he really could not stay. "I only stopped to
ask my way," he said.

But she would not hear of his leaving. "In the morning will
be time enough. It's dark; you would not be able to see the
path. Supper is ready, and it's a cold night."

So Saint Peter stayed, and the next morning he thanked
her. "I cannot pay you," he said, "but whatever you do first
tomorrow will last all day."

The woman fairly danced with joy. She ran back into the
house. "He said that whatever I do first tomorrow will last

all day! This is what I hoped for! Oh, that foolish widow—measuring cloth! *I* will count money. There will be so much money before the end of the day that we shall be rich forevermore! First, though, I must make bags to put it in. If I get up right after midnight to make the bags I can begin counting my money by daybreak."

She could hardly sleep for excitement. As soon as the clock struck midnight she leaped out of bed and put on her clothes and grabbed her scissors. She would have to work fast to make enough bags to hold all the money she intended to count.

As soon as she had cut up some old material she began on another piece, and when she had enough pieces she decided to sew them up at once. But, oddly enough, she couldn't stop cutting! She took the sheets off the bed and cut them up, and the curtains from the windows. Her husband cried out, "Woman, have you gone crazy?"

"I can't stop!" she answered him. "I can't keep these scissors from cutting!"

She cut up the bedspreads and the rugs and the tablecloths. She cut up her petticoats. Then she took her husband's suits, one by one, and cut those to pieces. The poor man ran about, begging her to stop, but nothing could stop her. She snipped off her bonnet strings and then cut up the bonnet itself. She opened her wardrobe and cut up all her dresses. The napkins went next, and the towels, and the aprons and the downstairs curtains. She wept in anger; her husband was bellowing with rage. But all day long, as long as there was anything to cut, she cut it up.

"Now I know what that stranger meant!" he shouted at her. "The first thing you did today—and you, you stupid woman, began the minute after midnight!"

He fled up the stairs to save the shirt he was wearing from her scissors. And all *she* had left, when midnight struck again,

was the dress she had on. The house was a shambles; all their fine things were cut to pieces. And instead of piles of money filling the rooms, they had only piles of rags and bits and pieces of clothing.

When the people in the village heard what had happened, they said, "It serves her right—and her husband, too, for having such a greedy wife." But what made her husband angriest of all was that, besides being so greedy, she had been so stupid.

THE HIPPOCRENE LIBRARY OF FOLKLORE

Czech, Moravian and Slovak Fairy Tales
Parker Fillmore

Everyone loves a "Story that Never Ends". . . Such is aptly titled the very last story in this authentic collection of Czech, Moravian and Slovak fairy tales, that will charm readers young and old alike. Fifteen different classic, regional folk tales and 23 charming illustrations whisk the reader to places of romance, deception, royalty, and magic.
Ages 12 and up • 243 pages • 23 b/w Illustrations • 5½ x 8 ¼ • 0-7818-0714-X • W • $14.95 hc • (792)

Fairy Gold: A Book of Classic English Fairy Tales
Chosen by Ernest Rhys
Illustrated by Herbert Cole

"The Fairyland which you enter, through the golden door of this book, is pictured in tales and rhymes that have been told at one time or another to English children," begins this charming volume of favorite English fairy tales. Forty-nine imaginative black and white illustrations accompany thirty classic tales, including such beloved stories as "Jack and the Bean Stalk," "The Three Bears," and "Chicken Licken."
Ages 12 and up • 236 pages • 5½ x 8½ • 49 b/w Illustrations • 0-7818-0700-X • W • $14.95 hc • (790)

Folk Tales from Bohemia
Adolf Wenig

This folk tale collection is one of a kind, focusing uniquely on humankind's struggle with evil in the world. Delicately ornate red and black text and illustrations set the mood. "How the Devil Contended with Man," "The Devil's Gifts," and "How an Old Woman Cheated the Devil" are just 2 of 9 suspenseful folk tales which interweave good and evil, magic and reality, struggle and conquest.
Ages 9 and up • 98 pages • red and black Illustrations • 5½ x 8¼ • 0-7818-0718-2 • W • $14.95 hc • (786)

Folk Tales from Chile
Brenda Hughes

This selection of 15 tales gives a taste of the variety of Chile's rich folklore. There is a story of the spirit who lived in a volcano and kept his daughter imprisoned in the mountain, guarded by a devoted dwarf; there are domestic tales with luck favoring the poor and simple, and tales which tell how poppies first appeared in the cornfields and how the Big Stone in Lake Llanquihue came to be there.
Ages 7 and up • 121 pages • 5½ x 8½ • 15 Illustrations • 0-7818-0712-3 • W • $12.50 hc • (785)

Folk Tales from Russia
by Donald A. Mackenzie

From Hippocrene's classic folklore series comes this collection of short stories of myth, fable, and adventure—all infused with the rich and varied cultural identity of Russia. With nearly 200 pages and 8 full-page black-and-white illustrations, the reader will be charmed by these legendary folk tales that symbolically weave magical fantasy with the historic events of Russia's past.
Ages 12 and up • 192 pages • 8 b/w Illustrations • 5½ x 8¼ •0-7818-0696-8 • W • $12.50 hc • (788)

Folk Tales from Simla
Alice Elizabeth Dracott

From Simla, once the summer capital of India under British rule, comes a charming collection of Himalayan folklore, known for its beauty, wit, and mysticism. These 56 stories, fire-side tales of the hill-folk of Northern India, will surely enchant readers of all ages. Eight illustrations by the author complete this delightful volume.

Ages 12 and up • 225 pages • 5½ x 8½ • 8 illustrations • 0-7818-0704-2 • W • $14.95 hc • (794)

Glass Mountain: Twenty-Eight Ancient Polish Folk Tales and Fables
W.S. Kuniczak
Illustrated by Pat Bargielski

As a child in a far-away misty corner of Volhynia, W.S. Kuniczak was carried away to an extraordinary world of magic and illusion by the folk tales of his Polish nurse. "To this day I merely need to close my eyes to see . . . an imaginary picture show and chart the marvelous geography of the fantastic," he writes in his introduction.

171 pages • 6 x 9 • 8 illustrations • 0-7818-0552-X • W • $16.95 hc • (645)

The Little Mermaid and Other Tales
Hans Christian Andersen

Here is a near replica of the first American edition of 27 classic fairy tales from the masterful Hans Christian Andersen. Children and adults alike will enjoy timeless favorites including "The Little Mermaid," "The Emperor's New Clothes," "The Little Matchgirl," and "The Ugly Duckling." Beautiful black-and-white sketches enhance these fairy tales and bring them to life.

Ages 9 and up • 508 pages • b/w illustrations • 6 x 9 • 0-7818-0720-4 • W • $19.95 hc • (791)

Old Polish Legends
Retold by F.C. Anstruther
Wood engravings by J. Sekalski

This fine collection of eleven fairy tales, with an introduction by Zymunt Nowakowski, was first published in Scotland during World War II, when the long night of the German occupation was at its darkest. The tales, however, "recall the ancient beautiful times, to laugh and to weep . . ."

66 pages • 7¼ x 9 • 11 woodcut engravings • 0-7818-0521-X • W • $11.95 hc • (653)

Pakistani Folk Tales: Toontoony Pie and Other Stories
Ashraf Siddiqui and Marilyn Lerch
Illustrated by Jan Fairservis

In this collection of 22 folk tales set in Pakistan, are found not only the familiar figures of folklore—kings and beautiful princesses—but the magic of the Far East, cunning jackals, and wise holy men. Thirty-eight charming illustrations by Jan Fairservis complete this enchanting collection.

Ages 7 and up • 158 pages • 6½ x 8½ • 38 illustrations • 0-7818-0703-4 • W • $12.50 hc • (784)

Polish Fables: Bilingual Edition
Ignacy Krasicki
Translated by Gerard T. Kapolka
   Ignacy Krasicki (1735-1801) was hailed as "The Prince of Poets" by his contemporaries. With great artistry the author used contemporary events and human relations to show a course to guide human conduct. This bilingual gift edition contains the original Polish text with side-by side English translation.
105 pages • 6 x 9 • 20 illustrations • 0-7818-0548-1 • W • $19.95 hc • (646)

Swedish Fairy Tales
Translated by H. L. Braekstad
   A unique blending of enchantment, adventure, comedy, and romance make this collection of Swedish fairy tales a must-have for any library. With 18 different, classic Swedish fairy tales and 21 beautiful black-and-white illustrations, this is an ideal gift for children and adults alike.
Ages 9 and up • 190 pages • 21 b/w illustrations • 5½ x 8¼ • 0-7818-0717-4 • W • $12.50 hc • (787)

Tales of Languedoc from the South of France
Samuel Jacques Brun
   For children to older adults (and everyone in between), here is a masterful collection of folktales from the South of France. Thirty-three beautiful black-and-white illustrations throughout bring magic, life, and spirit to such classic French folk tales as "My Grandfather's Tour of France," "A Blind Man's Story," and "The Marriage of Monsieur Arcanvel."
Ages 12 and up • 248 pages • 33 b/w sketches • 5½ x 8¼ • 0-7818-0715-8 • W • $14.95 hc • (793)

Twenty Scottish Tales and Legends
Edited by Cyril Swinson
Illustrated by Allan Stewart
   Twenty enchanting myths take the reader to an extraordinary world of magic harps, angry giants, mysterious spells and gallant Knights. Eight detailed illustrations by Allan Stewart bring the beauty of the Scottish countryside to the collection.
Ages 9 and up • 215 pages • 5½ x 8½ • 8 b/w illustrations • 0-7818-0701-8 • W • $12.50 hc • (789)

Ukrainian Folk Tales
Marie Halun Bloch
Illustrated by J. Hnizdovsky
   Many of the ingredients of folk tales, as well as some surprising Slavic twists, can be found in this unique and merry collection of 12 Ukrainian folk tales. Twenty-four witty and decorative wood-cut illustrations from J. Hnizdovsky complete the charm of the collection.
Ages 7 and up • 76 pages • 5½ x 8½ • 24 illustrations • 0-7818-0744-1 • $12.50 hc • W • (83)

Prices subject to change without prior notice. **To purchase Hippocrene Books** contact your local bookstore, call (718) 454-2366, or write to: HIPPOCRENE BOOKS, 171 Madison Avenue, New York, NY 10016. Please enclose check or money order, adding $5.00 shipping (UPS) for the first book and $.50 for each additional book.